THE WITCHING GAME

THE WITCHING GAME

ANNETTE CASCONE and GINA CASCONE

A TOM DOHERTY ASSOCIATES BOOK • NEW YORK

THE WITCHING GAME

A Starscape Book
Published by Tom Doherty Associates, LLC
175 Fifth Avenue
New York, NY 10010

www.tor-forge.com

ISBN 978-0-7653-3066-6

First Edition: March 2012

Printed in February 2012 in the United States of America by RR Donnelley, Harrisonburg, Virginia

0 9 8 7 6 5 4 3 2 1

For David and Scott
May all your wishes come true

THE WITCHING
GAME

1

"Aaaaggghhhh!"

Lindsey Jordan was dead. Dead, dead, dead! And she knew it. There was no place to run and no place to hide. In fact, if Lindsey hadn't tried to escape the horror in the first place, none of this would have happened. But now the horror was running loose through the house—along with a friend. And Lindsey was no longer locked inside the safety of her own room.

"Oh, man!" Lindsey's friend Bree Daniels gasped when Lindsey finally stopped screaming. "Your mother's going to kill us if she sees this mess! We'd better clean it up. And fast."

"No way," Lindsey snarled. "We didn't make this mess, so we're not going to clean it up." She stormed out of the living room into the foyer. Then she screamed up to the horror at the top of the stairs. "Alyssa!" she yelled at the top of her lungs. "Get down here right this minute, you little beast! And bring your sticky friend with you!"

Lindsey was answered by the sound of four little feet racing across the hallway upstairs.

"Alyssa, I'm not fooling around," Lindsey hollered. "If you don't get your butt down here right now, I'm going to come up there and kick it!"

"Drop dead!" Alyssa screamed back. Then a door slammed upstairs.

"That's it," Lindsey said as she took the first step. "I've had it with that kid. I'm going to kill her."

Bree grabbed Lindsey's arm to stop her. "We don't have time to kill her. Your parents will be home any minute. And if they see that living room, they're going to blame us."

Bree had a point. After all, she and Lindsey were supposed to be in charge. Lindsey had sworn to her parents that she and Bree were mature enough to be left alone with a couple of seven-year-olds. Little did they know that it would take a SWAT team to keep those brats under control.

"Don't you remember what your mother said?" Bree went on. "Watching them does not mean just being in the house. It means *watching* them."

To be honest, they hadn't been doing much watching at all. In fact, Lindsey and Bree had spent the entire afternoon locked up in Lindsey's room trying to escape the little horror and her friend. Lindsey needed the peace and quiet. Bree was helping her rehearse for the play tryouts the next day at school. They got so caught up in it that they actually managed to ignore the sounds coming from downstairs: the blaring TV, the screaming and giggling, the thumps and bumps, even the crashes.

They had forgotten all about the little horror and her partner in crime, Stephanie. That was a big mistake. Alyssa and Stephanie had turned the living room into a giant disaster area. Furniture was tipped over. The cushions were off the sofa and chairs. And what looked like every blanket in the house was draped across the mess to create a room-sized tent.

"This is unbelievable," Lindsey groaned as she and Bree walked back into the living room.

"It's not really that bad," Bree lied. "All we've got to do is fold up the blankets and fix up the furniture."

But they soon found out that that *wasn't all* they had to do.

Under the blankets, inside the tent, 128 crayons were scattered across the floor, along with every piece of every board game in the house. Stickers were stuck on everything—except the two dozen sticker books that littered the room. And in the center of it all, Alyssa's dolls were having a beach party—in a pile of sand art.

Somehow, Lindsey and Bree managed to clean the mess up. And they did it in record time. So what if the marbles from Hungry, Hungry Hippos were in the Monopoly box and Barbie's and Crystal's heads were in the trunk of the Dream Mobile? The room looked almost the way it had when Lindsey's parents left, and that was the important thing.

Bree heaved a sigh of relief as she turned off the vacuum. "I can't believe we got it all cleaned up before your parents got home."

"Yeah," Lindsey agreed. "And we've still got time to kill Alyssa." She headed into the foyer again. But before she turned to go up the stairs, she noticed something she'd missed before. The mirror on the wall across from the stairs was smeared with globs of peanut butter and jelly. "Look at this," she said to Bree in disgust. "No wonder that Stephanie kid is always so sticky."

"Do you want me to go get the glass cleaner?" Bree asked, exhausted.

"No," Lindsey answered, taking the steps two at a time. "We'll clean it up after those two little urchins are dead."

Lindsey was about to scream out to let Alyssa and her friend know what they were in for, but then she thought better of it. Why give them any warning? This would be a surprise attack.

"Shh," she whispered to Bree as they reached the top of the stairs.

They crept down the hallway toward Alyssa's room,

checking to make sure that all the other rooms were still intact. They paused at Alyssa's doorway and then burst through like a couple of TV cops about to make a bust.

But the little horror was nowhere to be found.

"Where the heck did they go?" Bree said. "And what destructive thing are they doing now?"

Lindsey raced back out into the hallway in a panic. As she was trying to decide where to look first, the sound of little voices caught her attention. The sound was coming from the room across the hallway—her parents' room. She gestured for Bree to follow her.

Luckily, the bedroom was in order. But it appeared to be empty—until more chattering led Lindsey straight to her parents' bathroom door. "They're in there," she whispered to Bree, pointing at the closed door.

"What are they doing?" Bree whispered back.

Before Lindsey could even venture a guess, Alyssa herself answered the question.

"Okay, I'm going to light the candle now." Her voice drifted through the door. "Then we'll turn out the light and say the chant."

"She's got matches in there!" Bree gasped, reaching for the doorknob.

Lindsey put a hand out to stop her. "They're playing Bloody Mary," she whispered to Bree. "Let's scare the living daylights out of them."

Inside the bathroom, Alyssa was explaining the rules of the game to Stephanie. "Now we have to stare at the mirror really hard, and watch carefully for Bloody Mary. Once we say the chant, she'll appear. But only for a second. As soon as she appears, I'll make the wish. Then Bloody Mary will make it come true. Ready?"

Lindsey heard the click that told her the bathroom lights were out. There were no windows in her parents' bathroom, so Lindsey knew it was dark inside. She could just picture Alyssa and Stephanie staring through the eerie glow of candlelight into the mirror above the sink. She and Bree smiled at one another as they heard the quivering voices begin the chant:

Bloody Mary is your name.
Please appear and play this game.
For the wish we ask of you,

You must make it now come true.
Once the wish has been revealed,
Can't turn back, its fate is sealed.
In return for what you give,
We will let your spirit live.

Lindsey and Bree paused for a second, imagining the two little urchins peering into the mirror expectantly. Then the older girls let out bloodcurdling screams. Before Lindsey and Bree had even stopped screaming, Alyssa and her friend began to wail inside the bathroom. Along with their cries came fumbling and bumping sounds. The doorknob turned, but Lindsey grabbed it and held the door shut.

Alyssa and Stephanie started pounding on the door. "Help us!" they screamed. "Somebody, help us!"

Lindsey and Bree were practically doubled over with laughter.

Finally, Lindsey let go of the doorknob and the door flew wide open, sending Alyssa and Stephanie toppling over each other onto the floor.

Lindsey had gotten her revenge. And she was feeling pretty pleased with herself.

Until she caught sight of the horrifying face in the mirror. And it wasn't Alyssa's.

2

Lindsey swallowed hard as she stood staring at the image glaring back at her. It was the reflection of a woman, a beautiful woman, dressed in black. But she hadn't appeared to grant any wishes. In fact, her dark, piercing eyes seemed to threaten a fate worse than death.

Terror tore through Lindsey's heart as the image started to speak.

"What in the world is going on in here?" Mrs. Jordan's voice was as strained as the reflection of her face in the mirror. She was standing in the doorway behind Lindsey and Bree, peering over their shoulders. This was truly a surprise attack.

Lindsey spun toward her mother. "Nothing, Mom," she lied.

Alyssa and her sticky friend scrambled to hide the matches and the candle.

"Then why was I greeted by screaming and yelling the moment I walked into this house?" Mrs. Jordan asked. "And what are the four of you doing playing in my bedroom?"

Alyssa shot Lindsey a pleading look. But Lindsey ignored it. "We weren't playing in your bedroom, Mom," Lindsey answered. "Alyssa and Stephanie were playing in your bathroom. Bree and I came in to drag them out."

Mrs. Jordan glanced down at Alyssa, who was now trying to shove the candle under the bathroom rug.

Lindsey smiled smugly. She was sure that her mother was about to blow a fuse, and that all the sparks would be flying in Alyssa's direction. She was only half right.

"Give me that candle," Mrs. Jordan snapped at Alyssa first.

Alyssa quickly handed it over.

"And the matches you're hiding," her mother demanded.

Again, Alyssa obeyed.

"How many times have I told you not to play with matches?" she scolded Alyssa.

"About a million?" Alyssa answered sheepishly.

"More like two," her mother said. Then the sparks flew in Lindsey's direction. "I thought I told you to watch the two of them," she said.

"I did," Lindsey lied. "But the minute I turned my back, they snuck up here to play Bloody Mary. Huh, Bree?"

Guilt flashed across Bree's face like a billboard advertisement, but she nodded yes.

"They're liars!" Alyssa accused. "They weren't watching us at all. They spent the whole day up in Lindsey's room practicing for Lindsey's stupid play tryouts while Stephanie and I sat on the couch all by ourselves, bored out of our minds. Huh, Steph?"

Now Stephanie nodded, looking just as guilty as Bree had.

Then the four girls exchanged dirty looks, but no one dared make another accusation. It would only land them *all* in more trouble.

Mrs. Jordan just shook her head in frustration.

"Hey." Another voice cut through the tension. "Doesn't anyone want to see what we bought at the auction?" It was Mr. Jordan, calling from the bottom of the stairs.

Mrs. Jordan's expression immediately changed. Whatever she and Mr. Jordan had bought at the auction must have been great, because all of a sudden Mrs. Jordan was smiling.

"Do you want to go see?" Mrs. Jordan's voice was full of excitement.

All four girls nodded, grateful to be off the hook. Then they followed Mrs. Jordan into the hallway.

"Is it a puppy?" Alyssa asked hopefully.

"You don't buy a puppy at an auction, you moron," Lindsey informed her.

"How do you know?" Alyssa shot back. "Maybe it was a puppy auction."

"It wasn't a puppy auction." Mrs. Jordan put an end to the bickering. "How many times do I have to tell you, Lyss, that we are not—read my lips, *not*—getting a puppy," she told her daughter firmly.

"Then what is it?" Alyssa grumbled as she followed her mother to the stairs.

"It's something for Lindsey's room," Mrs. Jordan answered.

"Bars, I hope," Alyssa whispered to Stephanie.

Mrs. Jordan shot her a look, but Alyssa didn't let up.

"How come you got something for Lindsey and not for me?" she complained.

Mrs. Jordan sighed. "Because your father and I just redid your entire bedroom, remember?"

Alyssa's room was full of brand-new furniture, not to mention new curtains and a fresh coat of paint.

Alyssa rolled her eyes as Lindsey smiled.

"So what is it, Mom?" Lindsey asked.

"You'll see," her mother answered, starting down the steps.

In the foyer, Mr. Jordan was cutting the twine off a huge package wrapped in brown paper. It stood at least six feet tall.

Lindsey couldn't begin to guess what it was. But she was dying to see. "Hi, Daddy," she called to her father as she bolted down the last few steps.

"Hey, guys." Mr. Jordan greeted them all. "I see everyone's still alive?" He raised his eyebrow at Mrs. Jordan.

Mrs. Jordan smiled back at him. "Barely," she said. Then she moved toward the package and started tearing off the brown paper like a little kid ripping into a birthday present. "Wait until you see this, Linds." Her voice promised something great.

Lindsey's excitement was growing—until the last piece of wrapping came off. Instead of oohing and aahing the way her mother wanted her to, Lindsey took a step back as if she were frightened.

Under the paper stood the most hideous thing Lindsey had ever seen. It was a floor mirror with a huge, dark wood frame. Snakelike carvings wrapped up the sides, leading to the head of what looked like a demon. The bottom looked like dragon's claws clutching ornately carved balls.

"So what do you think?" Mrs. Jordan wanted everyone to love it the way she obviously did.

"I don't know." Lindsey was trying to be tactful, but she gave Bree a look that said she hated it.

"It's old and dirty," Alyssa's sticky friend whispered loud enough for everyone to hear.

"And ugly," Alyssa added even louder. "It's perfect for Lindsey."

Mrs. Jordan's lips turned down. "For your information, young lady, this is a valuable antique. This mirror is more than a hundred years old."

"So what's that supposed to mean?" Alyssa was not impressed.

"That it's old, dirty, and ugly—and really expensive." Mr. Jordan winked at Alyssa.

"Oh, come on." Mrs. Jordan nudged him with her elbow. "It was a steal. Nobody else even bid on it."

"I hate to tell you this, Mom," Lindsey said, shaking her head, "but I can see why." Lindsey did not share her mother's enthusiasm for antiques. In fact, they gave her the creeps. To Lindsey, an antique was something that belonged to someone long dead.

"You're just being silly," Mrs. Jordan insisted. "This mirror is a spectacular work of art. Look at the detail."

Lindsey tried to seem interested as her mother

pointed out all the finely carved details. But her mind wandered from one creepy thought to the next.

Somebody dead owned this thing! Lindsey cringed. *And maybe someday when I'm long dead, some other mother will buy this mirror for her daughter because it's a valuable antique. Then my reflection will be frozen behind that glass with all its other dead owners.*

"You see how beautiful it is?" Her mother interrupted her thoughts.

Lindsey shook her head no. But her mother refused to give up.

"You'll see," she assured her. "Once it's all cleaned up and in your room, you're going to love it."

"Yeah," Lindsey whispered aloud. "To death."

3

The next morning, when Lindsey stood in front of the antique mirror, she was amazed.

The mirror itself still gave her the creeps, but the reflection inside it was perfect. Lindsey was amazed at how good she looked. She was amazed that the first outfit she put on was really the one she would wear. She was amazed that her hair came out just right for a change. Most of all, she was amazed that it all happened on a day when it was so important for her to look good.

She stared straight ahead into the strange, tinted glass, smiling at her reflection and peering deep into her dark brown eyes until she was almost in a trance.

A knock on the door broke the spell.

Lindsey turned away from the mirror as her mother came into the room. She couldn't help feeling a little embarrassed by her sudden vanity.

"I can't believe you're up and dressed already," Mrs. Jordan said, looking quite surprised.

"The auditions for the school play are today," Lindsey reminded her mother. "I wanted to be sure I looked just right."

"Well, I think you look perfect," Mrs. Jordan said.

"Thanks, Mom," Lindsey replied, turning to glance at herself in the mirror once again.

"Since you're all ready to go, you have plenty of time to eat a decent breakfast this morning," Mrs. Jordan said. "What would you like?"

"Can I have French toast?" Lindsey asked.

"Sure," her mother answered quickly, without pointing out how much extra work that was for her.

Lindsey soon found out why.

"And while I do that, why don't you straighten up your room." She sounded more pleasant than she usually did when she made that request.

Room cleaning was a definite sore spot between Lindsey and her mother. While Mrs. Jordan was a neat freak, Lindsey really hated cleaning. It was so boring. And pointless. Why waste time doing things like making the bed when you were just going to *un*make it again at night?

Lindsey had two choices. She could either start a rip-roaring fight with her mother first thing in the morning, or she could give in for a change.

She decided to pick option two. "All right," Lindsey said, rolling her eyes. "I'll straighten up."

"I'll call you when breakfast is ready." Her mother left, smiling like the cat who ate the canary.

Lindsey stood there looking around, wondering what to do first. She at least had to make it look as though she had tried to straighten up the room.

Finally she decided that the bed was a pretty logical place to start. She shuffled over to it and grabbed the edge of the comforter. She pulled it up and tried to smooth over the sheets, which were still in a tangled mess underneath. She flattened the lumps as best she could, tossed the pillows on, and considered it a job well done.

Next, she went to her desk, intending to shove all the clutter into a drawer so that the desktop would be neat without her having to go through all the junk. But when she opened the drawer, a packet of pictures caught her eye. She pulled them out and started flipping through them. They were pictures of Lindsey and her friends taken at the amusement park last summer.

There was one of her and Bree standing in line for the roller coaster. Then there was a shot of Tommy and Ralphie, her other best friends, making stupid faces at the camera. Next was a picture of all four of them screaming their heads off as they rode Rolling Thunder, the biggest roller coaster Lindsey had ever seen.

As she flipped through the stack of photographs, Lindsey started pulling out the ones she really liked. She would tape them to the new mirror. Since it was staying, the pictures would add a nice touch.

She fumbled through the pile of junk on her desktop and came up with a roll of tape, then headed over to the mirror and began arranging pictures. She taped up a half dozen of them, then stood back to admire her work.

But her eye was drawn away from the pictures and

into the mirror itself. Once again, Lindsey was peering deep into her reflection.

She might have stood there forever if her mother hadn't called her to come down for breakfast.

When Lindsey finally managed to tear herself away from the mirror, she realized that she hadn't done much to straighten up her room.

She hurriedly swept the mess on her desk into the open drawer, packed it down, and forced the drawer shut. She gathered up the dirty clothes that were strewn all over the floor and shoved them under her bed. Then she grabbed her books and headed out of her room.

Behind Lindsey, a drop of blood began to bead up on the mirror. And as it trickled down the glass, the pictures that Lindsey had taped to the wood fell to the floor.

4

Lindsey still felt confident when she and Bree went into the auditorium after school for the play tryouts. Thanks to all their rehearsing, Lindsey knew every line of the play, inside and out. She was excited about the possibility of winning the lead—until she saw who was sitting in the front row, waiting to audition.

"Oh, puke," Bree whispered the moment she caught sight of Lindsey's competition. "Look who's kissing up to Mr. Kreeger again."

The person playing up to the drama coach was Carolyn Berger, a blond-haired, blue-eyed, brown-nosing, two-faced show-off who loved to be in the spotlight.

Mr. Kreeger, the drama coach, thought she was perfect. So did every other teacher in school. But Lindsey and her friends knew better. Carolyn Berger was nothing but trouble. In fact, she brought trouble with her wherever she went. "Trouble" was a short, hostile bully with frizzy red hair and black stretch pants—a girl named Nancy Patanski. Trouble was sitting right next to Carolyn, eating a Twinkie.

A million butterflies suddenly took flight in Lindsey's stomach. "I don't even know why I'm bothering to try out for the lead," she told Bree. "Carolyn's going to get that part no matter what I do."

"That's not true," Bree said. "You're much better than Carolyn. Besides, you've got all the lines memorized already. Carolyn can barely remember her own name."

Just then, four waving arms in the center of the auditorium caught Lindsey's eye. Immediately she headed toward them, with Bree at her heels.

The arms belonged to Tommy and Ralphie. They were sitting in the middle row, waiting for Lindsey and Bree.

"Where the heck were you guys?" Tommy asked as

Lindsey and Bree plopped themselves down in the seats next to Ralphie. "You missed the whole thing!"

"What whole thing?" Lindsey asked, alarmed.

"The fight between the pit bull and Ralphie," Tommy answered.

The pit bull wasn't a dog—it was Nancy Patanski.

"No way!" Bree cried, clearly disappointed to have missed the fireworks. Next to Carolyn, Nancy Patanski was her least favorite person on earth.

"Yes, way!" Tommy laughed. "And Mr. Kreeger almost threw Nancy out of here, until Carolyn begged him to let her stay."

"You're kidding," Lindsey said. "What happened?"

"Tell them, Ralphie," Tommy ordered.

"She attacked me like a dog with rabies," Ralphie said, grinning from ear to ear, "for no reason at all."

For Ralphie, "no reason at all" was just another way of saying that he hadn't been the one who'd been caught in the act—whatever that was.

"What did you do?" Lindsey wanted to know.

Ralphie shrugged as if he didn't know. But Tommy started to explain.

"Nancy was going off about how she couldn't wait to see your audition, and how she and Carolyn were going to try really hard not to laugh in your face," he told Lindsey. "Then Ralphie told Nancy that Carolyn had about as much talent as his toenails, and that there was no way they were going to be laughing, because you were definitely going to kick Carolyn's butt. Huh, Ralphie?"

Ralphie nodded.

"Then he told Nancy that *her* butt was way too big for her pants," Tommy added.

"That's when she punched me," Ralphie announced proudly.

"Yeah," Tommy went on. "But all Mr. Kreeger saw was Nancy swinging her arms like a maniac and calling Ralphie all kinds of names."

"Way to go!" Bree gave Ralphie the high five.

Lindsey couldn't help but laugh. Nancy Patanski was just about the meanest kid in school. Even the teachers knew that.

Nancy was always picking on people—who were always half her size. Problem was, none of the teachers ever believed that Carolyn Berger was the one who instigated the fights. In fact, they were always praising Carolyn for trying to be a "positive influence" on Nancy. As long as Carolyn jumped to Nancy's defense, the teachers would let Nancy slide.

Little did they know that Nancy Patanski really was Carolyn Berger's personal guard dog.

"All I know is that you better kick Carolyn's butt," Ralphie told Lindsey. "Otherwise, Nancy's going to be totally vicious."

"For real," Tommy agreed. "She might even try to bite you," he told Ralphie. "And she probably does have rabies."

"Don't worry about it," Bree said. "Lindsey's going to get this part."

Lindsey appreciated the vote of confidence, and she was grateful to her friends for cheering her on, but thanks to Ralphie, the pressure was building. In fact, the fluttering in her stomach gave way to what felt like the barrel of a cement truck churning—especially when she was called to the stage.

You can do this, Lindsey assured herself as Mr. Kreeger

told her which part he wanted her to read. And while Mr. Kreeger seemed impressed when Lindsey informed him that she could do it by heart, Nancy Patanski started to growl and Carolyn Berger started to giggle.

It took every ounce of concentration Lindsey had to focus on her friends and not Carolyn and the pit bull as she began her audition.

Amazingly, though, the moment Lindsey opened her mouth, she stopped feeling nervous. The lines were rolling off her tongue with incredible ease, and she didn't miss a single word.

It was the best acting Lindsey had ever done. So good that Tommy, Ralphie, and Bree weren't the only ones who applauded wildly when she finished. So did Mr. Kreeger.

But he applauded even louder for Carolyn ten minutes later.

Still, Tommy, Ralphie, and Bree were convinced that Lindsey had won the part. And they told her as much over and over again as the four of them headed to her house, where they always went after school. The

Jordans' was the first stop along the way home, and the kitchen was always packed with snacks.

While Tommy and Ralphie raided the cabinets like a couple of locusts, Bree told Mrs. Jordan the same thing the four of them had been telling Lindsey—the lead in the play was definitely hers.

Mrs. Jordan was thrilled. She even agreed to let Ralphie take the chips and dip out of the kitchen and up to Lindsey's room, something she hadn't allowed him to do since he had spilled an entire jar of red salsa on Lindsey's sparkling white comforter six months before.

The moment Ralphie stepped inside Lindsey's room, he practically jumped. "Geez, oh, man," he exclaimed, staring at the mirror. "What the heck is that thing?"

"It's a mirror, you idiot," Bree shot back, grabbing the jar of salsa before Ralphie spilled it again.

"That's what your parents bought you at the auction?" Tommy asked, crinkling his nose.

Lindsey nodded, noticing that the pictures she'd taped to the mirror were gone. *That's weird*, she thought. *What could have happened to them?*

A quick glance around the room gave her the answer. The clothes under her bed were gone, the floor had been vacuumed, and her bedsheets were changed. Her mother must have taken the pictures down while she was cleaning. Lindsey was sure of it. Especially when she saw them stacked on her desk.

"That thing's disgusting," Ralphie informed them, pointing to the mirror.

"I know," Lindsey said. "But my mother just loves it. She says it's a valuable antique."

"You know what that means, don't you?" Ralphie didn't wait for an answer. "It means that you've got a dead person's mirror. And that's pretty *shkee-vy*."

"Tell me about it," Lindsey agreed. "You should have seen it before it was polished. It was totally creepy."

"I thought you told me this mirror was growing on you," Bree said.

"Growing like what?" Tommy asked. "A fungus?"

Lindsey laughed. "I said it didn't look so terrible with all my pictures taped to it," she told Bree.

"So why did you take them down?" Bree asked.

"I didn't," she answered. "My mom must have taken them off."

"So why don't you just put them back up?" Tommy asked.

"Because she'll take them down again. She probably doesn't want any tape on the wood," she said.

"So glue them back up," Ralphie suggested.

Just then, the seven-year-old horror came crashing into the room.

"Don't you know how to knock?" Lindsey growled at Alyssa.

"If I knocked, you'd lock the door," Alyssa replied, undeterred.

"That's the point," Lindsey said.

"I'm bored," Alyssa announced, plunking herself down on the bed. "I want to play a game or something. And Mommy said you have to."

"Look, you little beast," Lindsey snapped. "We do not exist to amuse you. Now get out!" Lindsey went over to the door, ready to close it behind Alyssa.

Alyssa didn't budge.

Lindsey was about to start a war, but Tommy put a stop to it. "I'll play a game with you," he told Alyssa.

Lindsey rolled her eyes. Tommy was always nice to the beast. Lindsey was sure it was because Tommy didn't have to deal with a bratty little sister full time. He was an only child.

"What do you want to play?" Tommy asked.

"How about Monopoly?" Alyssa suggested.

"No way," Ralphie jumped in. "That game takes like eighty-seven hours. Pick something else."

"I know!" Alyssa exclaimed. "We can play Bloody Mary in Lindsey's disgusting new mirror."

"Pick again," Ralphie said. "Bloody Mary's a stupid game. I'd rather play Monopoly."

Lindsey shot him a dirty look. At least Bloody Mary was fast. "You just don't want to play Bloody Mary because it totally freaks you out," she told him.

It did, too. Even when they were little, Ralphie had hated anything that had to do with spirits or ghosts. He was the only kid in kindergarten who hated Halloween—because the costumes scared him.

"It does not," Ralphie lied.

"Does, too," Tommy needled.

Bree laughed. "Ralphie's too scared to play Bloody Mary," she told Alyssa.

"I am not," Ralphie lied again. "I just don't think you should mess around with heebie-jeebie stuff. That's all."

"It's just a game," Alyssa told Ralphie.

"I know it's a game," Ralphie said. "A dopey, stupid game. But if that's what you guys want to play, fine by me."

"Go get the candle," Lindsey told Alyssa.

Five minutes later, the curtains were drawn, the candle was lit, and the chant had begun in front of the creepy old mirror.

Bloody Mary is your name.
Please appear and play this game. . . .

The candle flickered, casting eerie shadows on the strange tinted glass.

For the wish we ask of you,
You must make it now come true.

Once the wish has been revealed,
Can't turn back, its fate is sealed. . . .

Lindsey, Tommy, and Bree exchanged amused looks—
Ralphie was clearly spooked.

In return for what you give,
We will let your spirit live.

For a moment, the room was so quiet, Lindsey could
practically hear Ralphie's heart pounding against his
chest. She was about to grab him to make him scream
the way she used to when they were little, but something suddenly startled her instead.

Something startled them all.

5

I wish I had a puppy!" Alyssa blurted out excitedly. Her sudden outburst was enough to make Lindsey jump.

Tommy and Bree gasped.

And Ralphie *did* let out a scream.

But Alyssa didn't flinch. She jumped to her feet and pressed her face against the mirror as if she were struggling to see something, or someone, inside it.

For a second, Lindsey did the same. But other than the flickering candlelight and the reflection of Alyssa's smushed face, there was nothing to see.

She glanced back at Ralphie, who looked like he

was about to pass out. Lindsey still had an opportunity to scare the daylights out of him again. And she was definitely going to do it.

"There she is!" Lindsey proclaimed, pointing to a shadow of light dancing across the mirror. "It's Bloody Mary!"

Ralphie jumped back so quickly, he practically landed in Tommy's lap.

Lindsey cracked up.

So did Tommy and Bree.

But Alyssa wasn't laughing at all. "That's not Bloody Mary," she informed Lindsey. "Bloody Mary is already gone. Didn't you see her?"

"Sure I saw her," Lindsey joked. "Look," she said, pointing away from the mirror. "She's standing right behind Ralphie!"

Ralphie spun around fast.

Tommy and Bree laughed even harder.

"Very funny," Ralphie griped. "Are we done playing this stupid game, or what?"

"It isn't a game," Alyssa exclaimed. "It's real! Bloody Mary is real! And I'm going to get a puppy!"

"Forget it, Lyss," Bree said as she pulled open the curtains and blew out the candle. "The joke's over."

"It's not a joke!" Alyssa insisted. "I saw her. I saw Bloody Mary!"

Lindsey could tell by Alyssa's voice that she wasn't joking. Alyssa sounded the same way she had when she claimed to have seen Rudolph the Red-Nosed Reindeer flying through the night sky last Christmas Eve. And while for six months Lindsey had repeatedly dragged Alyssa outside after dinner to point out the blinking red lights on the airplanes above, Alyssa refused to believe that she'd seen anything other than Rudolph's red nose.

Needless to say, Lindsey wasn't about to try to convince Alyssa that what she had seen in the mirror was a shadow, not Bloody Mary. There was no point.

Unfortunately, it took Tommy and Bree another ten minutes to figure that out.

"Look," Tommy finally sighed. "There is no Bloody Mary, Alyssa. It's just a dopey, stupid game—like Ralphie said."

Alyssa huffed.

"He's telling the truth," Bree said. "Besides, even if there was such a thing as a spirit in the mirror, no one gets wishes for free."

"Oh, yeah?" Alyssa snapped back. "Well, you're dopey and stupid, because I'm getting a puppy!" She stormed toward the door. "You'll see," she said. "You're all going to be sorry."

Alyssa was right—they were all going to be sorry.

6

So when do you think Bloody Mary will give me my puppy?" Alyssa asked the next morning as Lindsey walked her to her bus stop.

Lindsey couldn't believe it. This kid just wouldn't let up. "You're not getting a puppy, Lyss," she said. "Get it through your head. Bloody Mary does not exist."

"She does too," Alyssa insisted. "I saw her. And if you see her and make a wish, she has to make it come true. Those are the rules."

Lindsey shook her head. She had no desire to go through this routine again. Besides, Alyssa would find out soon enough that she was not getting a puppy—not by making a wish, anyway. Life just didn't work like that.

"You'll see," Alyssa told her as they neared the corner of the block. "My wish will come true."

Across the street, a group of children were lining up for the bus. Lindsey looked down the block and saw that the bus was on its way. As usual, she'd gotten Alyssa there without a moment to spare.

"Hurry up," Lindsey told Alyssa, picking up her pace.

But Alyssa was already ahead of her. "Look!" Alyssa exclaimed, pointing across the street. "It's my puppy!"

Lindsey looked and saw a small white furball at the end of the line of kids. He was looking right at Alyssa, happily wagging his tail.

"That's exactly the puppy I imagined when I made my wish!" Alyssa shrieked.

He was exactly the puppy Lindsey would have wished for, too. He looked just like the picture in their dentist's office of a scruffy white puppy in wire-rimmed glasses.

The puppy barked at them as they stood at the corner waiting to cross. It was as if he recognized them.

No way, Lindsey told herself. *I'm just imagining things.*

The puppy called to them again.

Oddly, none of the other children at the bus stop paid any attention to the puppy, even when he barked. It was as if they didn't know he was there.

"I have to go get him!" Alyssa screamed, jumping off the curb.

Lindsey quickly grabbed her little sister and held her back. "Don't you dare cross this street without me," she scolded. "Do you hear me? You're going to get yourself killed!"

The school bus passed in front of them, red lights flashing. A car coming from the other direction stopped, as did the car behind the bus.

Lindsey waited a second to be sure it was safe. "*Now* we can cross," she told Alyssa.

Alyssa raced across the street. Lindsey had to run to keep up with her.

The bus blocked Lindsey's view of the other children, and of the puppy.

"Where is he?" Alyssa cried as she passed behind the bus and leaped up onto the curb. She stood for a moment, looking around. "Where did he go?"

Lindsey came up beside her.

The puppy was gone.

Meanwhile, the other children were filing onto the school bus.

"Lyss, you've got to go," Lindsey told her sister, pushing her toward the door of the bus.

Alyssa resisted. "I want my puppy," she demanded, still looking around.

The last kid in line was stepping onto the bus.

"We haven't got time for this," Lindsey insisted. "You've got to get on that bus." She grabbed Alyssa's arm and started dragging her toward the door. She wasn't about to go home and explain to her mother why Alyssa had missed the bus.

"But I want my puppy," Alyssa cried.

"Are you coming?" the bus driver asked impatiently.

"Yes," Lindsey answered. "She's coming." She pushed Alyssa up the steps.

As the bus doors closed, trapping Alyssa inside, Lindsey heard barking again. She turned toward the sound. The puppy was again sitting there, right where she'd last seen him.

Lindsey blinked hard. She had to be imagining things. But when she opened her eyes, the puppy was still there.

Alyssa had seen him, too. "Don't go away," she screamed from the window beside her seat.

Lindsey looked back at Alyssa, who was hanging out the window of the bus. She knew that her little sister was not calling to her. Alyssa's attention was focused on the puppy.

"Wait for me!" Alyssa said as the bus pulled away from the curb and started moving down the street.

Lindsey watched it go. She was almost afraid to turn around and look at the puppy again. Something about that dog was very, very strange.

Was it at all possible that Alyssa's wish had come true? she wondered. Was that really Alyssa's puppy?

A sudden chill made Lindsey shiver at the very thought.

No! she told herself firmly. She refused to be caught up in Alyssa's childish fantasies. That puppy had nothing to do with them or Bloody Mary.

Lindsey heard one last bark as she watched the school bus turn the corner and disappear from sight. Then she swung around to face the dog.

But she saw him for only a second, before he disappeared into thin air.

7

Lindsey stood there, looking around. She walked over to the spot where the puppy had been. She looked around some more.

There was no sign of a puppy anywhere.

Lindsey tried to convince herself that her imagination was playing tricks on her. That had happened before.

But this was an awfully big trick.

And Alyssa had seen the puppy, too.

Something weird was going on. Maybe it *was* Bloody Mary.

"Lind-sey!" A voice in the distance startled her.

Lindsey spun toward the sound, half expecting to see Bloody Mary. Instead, she saw Bree coming down the street.

"What are you doing there?" Bree asked as she got closer. Lindsey wondered what to tell her friend. She didn't want Bree to think she was as crazy as she felt. Still, she couldn't keep it to herself. "The strangest thing just happened," she said as Bree came up beside her.

"What?" Bree asked, looking around as Lindsey had done.

"Remember how Alyssa wished to Bloody Mary for a puppy?"

Bree nodded.

"Well, there was a puppy right here just a few minutes ago when Alyssa and I got to the bus stop," Lindsey explained. "He was barking at us and wagging his tail."

"No way!" Bree said.

Now it was Lindsey who nodded.

"Where is he now?" Bree asked.

"That's the weird thing," Lindsey told her. "Once Alyssa got on the bus, he disappeared."

"What do you mean, he disappeared?"

"He disappeared," Lindsey repeated. "Into thin air!"

Bree crossed her arms and stared at Lindsey in disbelief.

"It sounds pretty stupid, doesn't it?" Lindsey asked.

"Yeah, it does," Bree agreed.

"But there was a puppy," Lindsey said, trying to assure herself of that fact as much as Bree.

"I'm sure there was," Bree said. "But I don't think it had anything to do with Bloody Mary. He probably just lives in the neighborhood and wandered away from home."

Lindsey thought about it for a second. Maybe it was a real puppy that lived in the neighborhood. And maybe she was just so freaked out that she imagined it had disappeared into thin air. "You must be right," Lindsey decided. At least Bree's explanation was logical.

But there was still something nagging away at Lindsey, something that told her it had everything to do with Bloody Mary.

"We'd better get a move on it," Bree said, starting to walk. "If we don't hurry, we're going to be late for school."

Their school was six blocks away. Lindsey glanced

at her watch and saw they had less than ten minutes to get there before the bell rang. It seemed as though she and Bree were cutting it closer and closer every morning.

"We'd better run," Lindsey said.

The two of them took off, forgetting all about Bloody Mary for the moment.

But all through the day, Bloody Mary kept creeping into Lindsey's thoughts.

"It's a game, Lindsey," Bree insisted when Lindsey brought it up again after their last class.

The two of them were standing in front of their lockers, collecting their things to go home.

"What are you guys talking about?" another voice asked.

It was Ralphie. He had the locker right next to Bree's.

"Bloody Mary," Bree replied.

"Bloody Mary?" Tommy repeated. He was standing beside Ralphie, waiting for him. "What about Bloody Mary?"

Lindsey didn't answer right away. She knew how

crazy the story sounded and thought maybe she should just keep it to herself.

But Bree wasn't about to let that happen. "Go ahead, tell them," she prompted.

So once again, Lindsey recounted the events of the morning, as the four of them headed out of the school building and began walking home.

"It was just a coincidence," Tommy said, when Lindsey had finished. He wasn't making fun of her. He sounded as if he was trying to calm her fears.

"I don't know." Ralphie quickly jumped into the conversation. "It sounds pretty spooky to me."

"Give me a break." Tommy backhanded Ralphie. "Everything sounds spooky to you."

"But it was spooky," Lindsey said, still feeling very uneasy about the whole thing.

"Bloody Mary is not real," Tommy told her. He said it in the same kind of voice Lindsey's father had used years before when he'd tried to convince her that there was not a monster living in the closet.

"I'm not so sure," Ralphie disagreed. "There are all

kinds of weird, supernatural things in the world. What if Bloody Mary is one of them? What if Alyssa really did see her?"

"Did *you* see her?" Tommy asked Ralphie.

"Well, now that I think of it, I might have," Ralphie answered. "I did see something in that mirror just before Alyssa made her wish."

"Oh, brother!" Tommy slapped his hand against his face as he shook his head in disbelief.

Bree laughed.

But Lindsey didn't. "Let's just drop it, okay?" she said, feeling foolish for having brought it up in the first place.

"So what do you guys want to do now?" Ralphie asked after a minute.

"Uh-duh," Tommy huffed. "We've got a big history test tomorrow, so I think we'd better study."

"Well, let's do it at Lindsey's house, so we can get some munchies," Ralphie suggested.

When they got to Lindsey's they found her mother in the living room. She was on her hands and knees with a bucket beside her, scrubbing a spot on the carpet.

"What are you doing, Mom?" Lindsey asked.

Her mother looked up from her work. "I'm trying to get pee out of the carpet," she muttered, sounding pretty unhappy. Then without further explanation, she went back to attacking the spot.

The four friends exchanged confused, amused looks.

"Who peed on the carpet?" Lindsey wondered, trying not to laugh.

"Don't ask," her mother told her.

But Lindsey got her answer anyway.

"Hey, guys," Alyssa said, beaming. "Look what I've got!"

Lindsey gasped loudly at the sight of what her sister held tightly in her arms.

It was a puppy—the same puppy they'd seen that morning at the bus stop.

8

Lindsey could feel the blood draining from her face as she stood there staring at the squiggling white furball in Alyssa's arms. "It's him!" she cried, grabbing Bree's shoulder. "It's the puppy from the bus stop!"

Every muscle in Bree's body went rigid and her eyes bulged out of her head.

Tommy stood stunned, as if he'd just seen a ghost.

And Ralphie jumped back so far and so fast, he practically landed in the foyer.

The puppy let out an excited yip.

Mrs. Jordan sighed. "I thought I told you that puppy

stays in the kitchen where he can't do any more damage," she scolded Alyssa.

"But I'm holding him, Mom," Alyssa protested.

"I don't care." Mrs. Jordan frowned. "Back in the kitchen."

Lindsey and her friends looked at one another in disbelief.

"I knew we should have left that puppy where we found him," Mrs. Jordan complained.

"And where was that?" Lindsey asked nervously.

"At the end of our driveway," Mrs. Jordan answered.

"He was waiting for me when I got home from school," Alyssa informed them, smiling from ear to ear.

"He was not waiting for you, Alyssa."

From the sound of her voice, Lindsey could tell that her mother had already been through this many times.

"The poor little guy is just lost," Mrs. Jordan continued. "And he's going right back to his owner, as soon as I can get a hold of her."

"His owner?" Lindsey repeated numbly. How in the world was her mother going to give this puppy back to a spirit in the mirror?

"Yes," Mrs. Jordan said. "His owner."

"By any chance is her name Mary?" Ralphie gulped.

"No," Mrs. Jordan replied. "It's someone named Millie. Millie Bishop. At least that's the name on the puppy's dog tags."

Lindsey looked at the puppy. There, under the fluffy white fur on his neck, was a brown leather collar. Dangling from the center of it was a silver tag. "He's real!" she exclaimed, heaving a sigh of relief. "The puppy is real!"

"He's real, all right," Mrs. Jordan groaned as she continued to scrub. "And so is the puddle he left on my carpet."

Lindsey let out a laugh. Then she reached out to pet the puppy's head. This wasn't a spooky spirit dog. It was a real dog with a real, live owner who had a real phone number. Suddenly, Lindsey couldn't resist him.

"You were right," she told Bree. "This poor little guy must live in the neighborhood somewhere. And he's probably too young to find his way home."

"Actually," Mrs. Jordan said, "he lives about five miles from here, in Robbinsville. How he wandered this far from his home is totally beyond me."

"He didn't wander," Alyssa told them. "He was looking for me."

Mrs. Jordan rolled her eyes in exasperation. "Yeah," she said. "Well, now Millie Bishop is looking for him. And as soon as I get her on the phone, we're dropping that dog off. So don't get attached. Until then, I want him back in the kitchen."

Lindsey was amazed when Alyssa didn't bother to put up a fight. She just turned around and headed for the kitchen, with Millie Bishop's puppy in tow.

Lindsey and her friends followed.

"He's not yours," Lindsey told Alyssa as the five of them played with the puppy, who was bouncing across the kitchen floor.

"He is, too," Alyssa insisted. "Bloody Mary gave him to me."

"Then she stole him from Millie Bishop," Ralphie chimed in.

Bree and Tommy laughed.

"I don't care what you guys think, or what Mommy says," Alyssa informed them. "This is my puppy. And I'm keeping him."

"What do we have to do to make you understand that there is no Bloody Mary?" Bree asked Alyssa.

"What do I have to do to make you understand that there is?" she shot back.

Even Tommy had had enough. "If there really is a Bloody Mary, how come none of us got our wishes when we were kids?" he asked Alyssa. "We played all the time."

"Who knows." Alyssa shrugged. "Maybe she likes me best."

"I doubt it," Lindsey said.

"I have an idea," Bree announced. "One that will prove to you that this puppy was just a coincidence, and that Bloody Mary is just a joke."

Lindsey knew exactly what Bree was thinking.

So did Ralphie, because he objected before Bree even finished her thought. "Forget it," he said. "We're not making another wish."

"Why not?" Tommy asked. "It's the only way to get it through this kid's head that wish-granting spirits just don't exist."

"Tommy's right," Bree told Ralphie. She turned to

Alyssa. "Hey, Lyss, if we make a wish that doesn't come true, you promise you'll forget all about Bloody Mary?"

Alyssa smiled. "Yup," she said. "And I'll even do whatever you guys tell me to do for three whole weeks."

Lindsey couldn't resist a bet like that, even though she knew Alyssa would never make good on it. "You've got a deal," she told her sister. "We'll play again, just like we did yesterday. But this time, you don't get to make the wish," she informed Alyssa. "This time, we're going to make a wish for all of us. And it's got to be something that couldn't possibly happen all by itself."

"Fine," Alyssa agreed.

"Let's wish for money—a hundred dollars each," Bree exclaimed.

"Good one," Lindsey agreed. "But let's make it two hundred each." Money was always hard to get. And she was pretty sure there was no way a thousand dollars was going to miraculously appear.

Tommy agreed, too. But Ralphie was still hemming and hawing about messing around with spirits as they dragged him out of the kitchen and up to Lindsey's room.

As Lindsey lit the candle, they all took their seats

in a semicircle around the old mirror. Before the chant began, Alyssa made them all swear that they would take the game seriously. She insisted that Ralphie make the wish because Ralphie was the only one who was *already* taking the game seriously.

Lindsey, Bree, and Tommy exchanged amused looks. But Ralphie sat stone-faced, reciting the chant as quickly as he could.

Bloody Mary is your name.
Please appear and play this game.
For the wish we ask of you,
You must make it now come true. . . .

Lindsey couldn't help snickering as Ralphie's voice started to crack.

Once the wish has been revealed,
Can't turn back, its fate is sealed. . . .

Lindsey quickly turned serious as Alyssa shot her a dirty look.

In return for what you give,
We will let your spirit live.

For a second, the thought of getting two hundred dollars had Lindsey hoping she really would see a spirit in the mirror. But when Ralphie finished the last line of the chant, all she saw were their familiar reflections.

By the looks of them, Tommy and Bree were hoping for two hundred bucks, too. They were both squinting intensely as they peered into the glass.

For a moment it was so quiet, Lindsey could hear her own heart beating—until Ralphie suddenly jumped to his feet.

"I wish I didn't have to take that stupid history test tomorrow!" he exclaimed, startling the rest of them.

Lindsey was sure that Ralphie was just trying to scare *them* for a change. But Ralphie was staring into the mirror as if he were in a trance. And before anybody could say anything, Alyssa was dancing around the room victoriously.

"See?" She stuck her tongue out at them. "Didn't I tell you?" Then she danced over to Ralphie and punched him in the arm. "Hey," she complained. "Why didn't you wish for the money, like we said?"

Ralphie spun around, looking totally spooked. "Something was in there," he said in a quivering voice.

"Yeah," Alyssa told him. "Bloody Mary!"

Lindsey, Tommy, and Bree stared at one another in disbelief, then they all turned suspiciously back toward Ralphie.

"Didn't you guys see anything?" Ralphie asked nervously.

"*Nooooooo,*" they answered at the same time.

"How could you have missed her?" Alyssa demanded. "She was right there," she said, pointing to the mirror. "She was even clearer than she was the last time, huh, Ralphie? You could see her face and her eyes and everything."

Ralphie was silent.

"Well?" Lindsey glared at Ralphie. "Could you?"

"I don't know," Ralphie finally answered. "It was all kind of blurry. But I definitely saw something."

"You're out of your mind," Tommy told him. "There was nothing in that mirror."

Lindsey and Bree exchanged worried glances.

"There was nothing in there," Tommy repeated as if they were all out of their minds.

"Yes, there was," Alyssa insisted. "And as soon as Ralphie gets his wish, you guys have to do everything I say for three whole weeks."

"What are you talking about?" Lindsey snapped, suddenly more irritated by her sister than freaked out by Ralphie.

"That was the deal," Alyssa told her.

"Was not. Nobody but you promised that," Lindsey said.

"Lindsey's right," Bree said. "You're the only one who made the deal."

"Oh, brother." Tommy laughed. "What difference does it make? Didn't you hear what Ralphie wished for? There's no way he's getting out of that test. He'd have a better shot at the money."

Tommy had a point.

But Bloody Mary had a plan.

9

It looks like your stupid wish isn't going to come true," Tommy grumbled at Ralphie as the four friends took their seats in class the next day.

Lindsey was actually a little relieved. It was way too creepy to think that they really had called up some kind of spirit. Still, at the same time, she was kind of disappointed. *Too bad*, she thought. *It would have been nice to have someone who really could make all our wishes come true.* But this was the proof that Bloody Mary just didn't exist.

Their teacher, Mrs. Wickley, was standing in front of her desk ready to pass out the test. Lindsey wished she'd spent more time studying and less time playing Bloody Mary. She was sure her friends felt the same way.

Ralphie looked especially disappointed. He'd really believed that he saw something in the mirror. "What are you complaining about?" he whispered to Tommy. "You sit next to Herbie Finkelstein. He's Mr. History Expert. All you've got to do is peek at his paper and you'll get an A."

"I'm not going to peek at Herbie Finkelstein's paper," Tommy protested.

Lindsey believed him, for two reasons. First, Tommy wasn't a cheater, and second, Herbie Finkelstein was one of those kids who covered his paper while he was writing so that no one else could see it.

"We're doomed," Bree said. "We're all going to fail. And it's all your fault," she told Ralphie.

Lindsey couldn't help feeling that it was partly her fault, too. After all, she'd been the one to start all this Bloody Mary nonsense.

Now they were really going to pay for it.

When all the kids in the classroom had taken their seats, Mrs. Wickley began walking up and down the aisles, passing out the tests. She put them on the desks facedown so that no one could begin reading until she said, "Start."

Ralphie groaned loudly when Mrs. Wickley put the test on his desk.

So did Mrs. Wickley.

She stopped walking and grabbed on to the edge of Ralphie's desk. "Oh, my goodness," she said, putting the stack of tests down and raising her hand to her forehead. "I don't feel very well all of a sudden."

"What's the matter, Mrs. Wickley?" Herbie Finkelstein jumped out of his seat and hurried to her aid.

"I—" Mrs. Wickley started. But she never finished answering Herbie's question. All of a sudden, Mrs. Wickley collapsed onto the floor in front of Ralphie's desk, limp as a rag doll.

10

"Call nine-one-one!" Herbie Finkelstein screamed hysterically. "Call nine-one-one! Mrs. Wickley's dead!" He ran out of the classroom into the hallway, repeating his message over and over again like the town crier.

The rest of the kids in the classroom remained glued to their seats, frozen in fear—especially Ralphie.

"What should we do?" Sandy Becker cried. She dug through her backpack and pulled out her cell phone. "*Should* we call nine-one-one?"

"I think we should get the principal," Mark Tyler said as he ran out of the classroom.

"Good idea," Tommy called out to him. Then Tommy got out of his seat and knelt down on the floor next to Mrs. Wickley. He picked up her hand and began patting it. "Mrs. Wickley! Wake up!"

"No way you killed Mrs. Wickley with your stupid wish," Bree whispered to Ralphie.

"Don't blame me," Ralphie told her. "I didn't wish for anything bad to happen to Mrs. Wickley. I just wished not to have to take the stupid test."

"What are you talking about?" Sandy Becker asked.

"Nothing," Lindsey said, trying to put a stop to the conversation. The last thing she wanted was to have to explain about Bloody Mary to the whole class.

"Mrs. Wickley!" Tommy shouted. "Can you hear me?"

Kenny Goodman, the class clown, came up with an idea. "Slap her face," he told Tommy.

"What?" Tommy was appalled.

"Slap her face," Kenny repeated. "They do it in the movies all the time to wake people up," he informed Tommy.

"I'm not slapping Mrs. Wickley!" Tommy was adamant.

Just then, the principal, Mr. Steele, came rushing into the room with Herbie Finkelstein and Mark Tyler behind him. Tommy got out of the way as the principal knelt down beside Mrs. Wickley.

"Everybody stay calm," Mr. Steele instructed. "Mrs. Wickley is going to be just fine." He lifted her head off the floor and gently patted her cheek.

"See?" Kenny Goodman shot Tommy a look. "I told you so."

Mrs. Wickley's eyes fluttered.

"She's coming around already," Mr. Steele assured the class.

"What happened?" Mrs. Wickley muttered.

"You just had one of your little episodes," the principal reassured her. "Mrs. Wickley has low blood sugar," he explained to the class. "If she doesn't eat properly, she has fainting spells."

Mrs. Wickley was sitting up now. "I'm so sorry," she said to the class. "I must have scared you kids half to death."

"Are you okay, Mrs. Wickley?" Herbie Finkelstein asked, still trembling.

"I'm fine, Herbie," she answered, getting to her feet. She was still pretty wobbly.

"I think you should come with me to the nurse's office," Mr. Steele said to Mrs. Wickley. "You should probably go home for the rest of the day. I'll send a substitute teacher in to take care of your class."

Mrs. Wickley didn't argue with him. "Thank you" was all she said as the principal helped her to the door.

"Everyone sit quietly in your seats, please," the principal instructed. "Someone will be here shortly. In the meantime, you will be in charge, Herbie."

"What about the test?" Herbie asked.

"No test today, Herbie," Mrs. Wickley said faintly. "We'll worry about it later in the week," she added as Mr. Steele guided her out the door.

"No test!" someone exclaimed once they were gone.

"What incredible luck!" Kenny Goodman added.

Lindsey, Bree, Tommy, and Ralphie exchanged nervous glances.

Luck had nothing to do with it.

11

Will everybody just calm down!" Tommy shouted above all the chatter. The four of them were standing by their lockers after school, obsessing about Bloody Mary. While Lindsey, Ralphie, and Bree were still freaked out over what had happened to Mrs. Wickley, they were beginning to feel pretty excited at the idea that there really was a wish-granting spirit living in Lindsey's mirror. But Tommy wasn't buying it.

"Mrs. Wickley's fainting spell was just a coincidence," he continued. "You heard Mr. Steele—she passes out all the time. It had nothing to do with Ralphie's wish."

"I don't know," Lindsey said. "It seems to me that

we're already two for two. Admit it, Tommy. Alyssa wished for a puppy, and bam"—Lindsey snapped her fingers—"she got one. Ralphie wished to get out of the test, and bam, we didn't have to take it."

"First of all," Tommy said, "Alyssa did not get a puppy. It belongs to somebody else. And second, we're still going to have to take that test as soon as Mrs. Wickley comes back."

"Darn it, Ralphie," Bree said, "you should have made your wish more clear. You should have said that you didn't want to take the test for the rest of your life!"

"For real," Ralphie agreed.

"No," Lindsey told him. "You should have wished for the money. Then we could have gone shopping at the mall. Imagine the kind of stuff we could have gotten with a thousand dollars!"

"Wait a minute!" Bree exclaimed. "We don't need any money. We could have anything we want anyway. All we have to do is wish for it!"

Even Ralphie was caught up in that idea. "This could be too cool," he said. "What do you think we should wish for next?"

"I thought you were afraid of all this 'heebie-jeebie' stuff," Tommy pointed out.

"I was," Ralphie admitted. "But Bloody Mary's obviously a good spirit. So what's the big deal?"

Tommy groaned.

"Oh, come on," Lindsey said. "Wouldn't it be great if it were true, if we really could get anything we wanted?"

"It's not true," Tommy insisted. "It's just wishful thinking."

"I say we test it out again," Bree suggested. "Then we'll know for sure."

"I say we drop it," Tommy told them. "Besides, Ralphie and I have baseball tryouts today."

Before Lindsey had a chance to protest, she was interrupted by Carolyn Berger and her Twinkie-eating pit bull.

"Hi, Lindsey." Carolyn affected a sugary-sweet voice.

"You mean 'loser,' don't you?" Nancy Patanski got in the first dig as she sank her fangs into her Twinkie.

Tommy and Ralphie exchanged irritated looks, as did Lindsey and Bree.

"Oh, come on, Nancy." Carolyn pretended to be

nice. "We don't know that Lindsey's a loser. The cast list hasn't been posted yet."

"Like it makes any difference," Nancy said. "We all know what the outcome will be."

Lindsey's stomach lurched. With all the excitement, she'd almost forgotten about the play. The cast list was going up first thing the next morning. And thanks to Carolyn, she suddenly remembered just how badly she wanted her name to be on it, right next to the part that was listed as "lead."

Still, she had no desire to get into a fight with the pit bull.

Ralphie did. In fact, he was already winding up for the punch.

But Bree beat him to it.

"Gee, Nancy." Bree imitated Carolyn's obnoxious tone. "I really love your pants. Too bad you can't breathe in them."

Ralphie, who was just about to start swinging, cracked up instead. "Good one, Bree."

"Yeah, Bree," Nancy said. "That was real funny. So

funny, I'm gonna rip your heart out." Nancy took a step forward as if she might try.

Bree didn't flinch. "Yeah, and what are you going to do with it? Eat it?"

Ralphie laughed even harder.

Just as Nancy was about to lunge forward, Mr. Steele came out of his office and into the hallway.

Carolyn quickly grabbed the pit bull by the collar and pulled her away. Then she and Nancy smiled innocently as Mr. Steele walked past them.

"Come on, Nancy." Carolyn's sweetness turned snippy. "There's no reason to pick on the loser and her pathetic friends now. We might as well wait until tomorrow."

"Yeah," Nancy said, "when they're *already* crying."

With that, Carolyn strutted down the hall, with Nancy clomping loudly beside her.

"You're the one that's going to be crying, Nancy," Bree screamed after them.

"In your dreams, cheese face," Nancy shot back.

"*Oooooohhhhh!*" Bree was fuming. "I hate that girl!"

"Just forget about it, Bree," Lindsey said as she opened her locker door. "They're only looking for trouble."

"Yeah," Bree agreed. "And I want to give it to them. Go down there and bite her or something, Ralphie," she begged.

"Why?" Ralphie asked. "You already got her good."

"Not good enough," Bree said. "I wish that one of these days somebody really *would* make Nancy Patanski cry."

Lindsey shook her head as she crammed her books into her locker. "It'll never happen," she said.

Just then, a loud *rrrr-iiiip* echoed through the hallway, as if someone were tearing a bedsheet.

But it wasn't a sheet. It was Nancy Patanski's pants.

Lindsey caught sight of them in the mirror hanging inside her locker door before she turned back around.

"Check it out!" Ralphie exclaimed, pointing at Nancy. She was bending over, picking up the Twinkie she'd dropped. The back of her pants had split right up the seam, and her giant underwear was sticking out of them. Only Nancy didn't know it—until every other kid in the hallway started to laugh.

"Hey, Nancy," one of the seventh graders called out. "Your butt's hanging out."

Nancy turned as red as a beet as she felt her behind.

"And today's not Wednesday, either," another kid added, reading the pink letters across Nancy's behind. "It's Thursday. Didn't your mommy tell you to change your underwear this morning?"

"No way, Nancy wears 'days of the week' underwear!" another kid said with a laugh.

Nancy burst into tears. Then she ran down the hallway trying to hold the seat of her pants together, with Carolyn scrambling to help.

Tommy, Ralphie, and Bree stood stunned, watching the scene in amazement. So did Lindsey—until she felt something touch the back of her shoulder. It felt like a thin, icy finger.

Lindsey spun around fast, expecting to see Mr. Steele, ready to scold them.

But it wasn't Mr. Steele. In fact, it was no one at all—at least not in person.

Still, the reflection was clear.

12

"Look!" Lindsey shrieked, pointing at her mirror.

But by the time her friends had turned around, the face in the mirror had disappeared.

"What is it?" Bree asked.

"I think I just saw Bloody Mary," Lindsey told her. "She was in my locker mirror."

"What was she doing in your locker mirror?" Bree wondered, stepping up to examine the mirror for herself.

Before Lindsey had a chance to answer, Ralphie butted in. "Are you sure it was her?" he asked. "What did she look like?"

Lindsey closed her eyes and tried to picture the glimpse she'd caught. "Dark hair," she said, conjuring up the image. "Her hair was very dark. And wild. It was really curly, all around her face."

"That's her all right," Ralphie said.

"I thought you said she was all blurry yesterday," Tommy reminded him.

"She was," Ralphie snapped. "But I remember seeing dark, curly hair."

"Sure you do," Tommy said, rolling his eyes.

Lindsey ignored them as she continued with her description. The more she pictured the face in the mirror, the more it freaked her out. "She had eyes as black as night. I couldn't tell whether she was looking at me or right through me."

"What was she doing in your locker mirror?" Bree repeated her question.

Lindsey just shrugged. She had no idea.

But Ralphie did. "You called her up," he said to Bree. "You said you *wished* that somebody would make Nancy cry. And somebody did."

"That's ridiculous," Tommy said.

"No, it isn't," Ralphie claimed.

"Are you saying that every time we make a wish now, Bloody Mary will appear and make it come true?" Bree asked, sounding a bit spooked—and a bit hopeful.

"Could be," Ralphie said. "At least whenever we're near a mirror."

"Then we'd better start being really careful about what we wish for when we're around mirrors," Tommy told them, trying to sound serious. But Lindsey could see from the look on his face that he was making fun of them. Even now, after everything that had happened, Tommy still believed it was all a coincidence.

"Are you crazy?" Ralphie asked. "Don't you see what this means? We really *can* have anything we want just by wishing for it."

Tommy laughed in Ralphie's face. "I don't think I'm the crazy one here," he said.

"Ralphie's right," Lindsey insisted. "Bree made a wish. And now we're three for three."

"Which is just about the age you're acting," Tommy retorted.

"You know what I think?" Bree said, ignoring Tommy.

"I think we ought to try it again. Right here. Right now."

"In the locker mirror?" Ralphie asked.

"Why not?" Bree answered. "She was here just a minute ago."

"We can't," Lindsey said. "What if somebody hears us saying the chant? They'll think we're crazy. Besides, we don't have a candle."

"What do you need a candle for?" Tommy teased. "If Bloody Mary really did rip Nancy's pants to make her cry, you don't even need to say the chant anymore. In fact, you don't even have to look into the mirror. Bree didn't."

"Tommy's right," Ralphie said. "Let's just do it without the chant and see what happens."

Tommy looked like he was about to scream. "You want to know what'll happen?" he snapped at Ralphie. "Nothing will happen. Watch." Tommy pressed his nose against the glass on the door. "I wish that Ralphie would shut up for good!"

"What kind of stupid wish is that?" Ralphie griped.

"You see?" Tommy said, turning to Lindsey and Bree.

"It didn't work. And there's no one in that mirror but me."

"Let me try," Ralphie said, shoving Tommy out of the way. "I wish Tommy would get a split in *his* pants—and his underwear, too!"

Tommy rolled his eyes. But the seam in his pants stayed put. "I'm going to baseball tryouts," Tommy announced, laughing at the three of them.

Ralphie tried another wish, but when he looked down, his feet were still in his dirty old sneakers, not shiny new cleats.

A few yards down the hall, Tommy turned back around. "Hey, Ralphie," he called. "If I were you I'd be wishing for a place on the girls' swim team. Because if you don't show up for baseball today, that's the only team that's still having tryouts."

"Shoot." Ralphie reacted immediately. "I have to go. We'll try to reach Bloody Mary later, at Lindsey's house," he told them. "She probably flew back to that mirror or something."

Lindsey just shrugged. Anything was possible.

"But don't play without me," Ralphie shouted as he

rushed off to catch up with Tommy. "I definitely want in on the next wish."

"You already got a wish," Bree told him.

"Well, so did you," Ralphie shot back.

"Don't worry, Ralphie," Lindsey said, trying to keep peace. "We'll wait for you."

"Promise?" Ralphie asked.

"Promise," Lindsey assured him as she and Bree headed off in the other direction, toward the exit.

On their walk home, Lindsey and Bree talked about all the things they would wish for.

The conversation quickly got out of control. Before long, the two of them were giggling about making impossible wishes—like becoming movie stars, and having a million dollars, and knowing everything in the world without ever going to school again, and having all the candy in the universe.

Bloody Mary was just too good to be true.

As Lindsey and Bree turned onto their street, they ran into Alyssa. She was walking toward them. The puppy trotted along beside her on a leash.

"What are you doing, Lyss?" Bree asked.

"I'm taking *my* puppy for a walk," she answered.

The way Alyssa exaggerated the word "my" and the way she was smiling told Lindsey that something was up.

Alyssa was so excited that she spilled the beans before Lindsey could even ask what it was. "I get to keep the puppy!" she exclaimed.

"But what about his owner?" Lindsey asked.

"Well, it's kind of a long story," Alyssa told her.

Nothing was worse than having to listen to Alyssa's long stories. "Tell me the short version," Lindsey said.

"Okay." Alyssa shrugged. "His owner is a very old lady. Her daughter got her the puppy as a birthday present, to keep her company, because her daughter lives out of town. But the other day, the puppy tripped the old lady, and she fell down the steps and broke her hip. Now she's in the hospital, and she's not going to be able to take care of the puppy."

"How did you find all this out?" Lindsey wanted to know.

"Mommy kept calling the phone number that was on his tag," Alyssa explained. "She must have left twelve messages. Finally, somebody called Mommy back. It was another old lady. She told Mommy the whole story. And she said that we could keep the puppy if we promised to take good care of him."

"What did your mother say about all this?" Bree asked.

"She said he's all mine." Alyssa smiled as she bent down to scoop up the puppy. "Didn't she, Wishes?"

Bree shot Lindsey an amused look as Alyssa kissed the puppy on the nose. "You named the puppy Wishes?"

"Uh-huh." Alyssa was gloating. "I told you Bloody Mary would give me a puppy."

Suddenly, Lindsey wasn't so sure she wanted to make another wish. Every time one came true, something bad seemed to happen—to somebody else.

13

"No more Bloody Mary!" Lindsey and Bree agreed.

They made Tommy and Ralphie go along with them, too.

Lindsey, Bree, and Ralphie thought the whole thing was just too dangerous.

Tommy still thought the whole thing was nonsense. But he said he'd be happy if he never had to hear about it again.

So they promised not to talk about it anymore. They were going to forget all about Bloody Mary.

But that was easier said than done.

That night when Lindsey went to bed, she had an

impossible time trying to fall asleep. She kept playing the fight with Carolyn and Nancy over and over in her head. She was terrified that Nancy was right, that Carolyn was going to get the lead in the play.

Lindsey tossed and turned until well after midnight, worrying herself sick about what would happen the next day at school. The later it got, the more convinced she became that she was not going to get the part. She might be able to deal with the disappointment of that, but there was no way she would be able to bear the humiliation she would suffer at the hands of Carolyn and the pit bull.

Suddenly, a flicker of light seemed to dance across the surface of Lindsey's mirror.

What is that? she wondered, staring into the glass. But the light was gone. She decided it must have been the reflection of something outside.

As she continued to lie in bed with her eyes fixed on the mirror, a little voice inside her head told her to wish to Bloody Mary to get the part.

No! she told herself firmly. But she couldn't turn away from the mirror. It seemed to be calling to her.

What harm could it do? the little voice said.

Lindsey thought about what had happened to the old lady who owned the puppy. And Mrs. Wickley. And Nancy.

"No Bloody Mary," Lindsey told herself out loud.

But the little voice piped up again. *The old lady will get better. Mrs. Wickley is fine; she just has low blood sugar. And Nancy deserved what she got. So what's the big deal?*

What *was* the big deal? If wishing to Bloody Mary could win Lindsey the part, who would it hurt?

Carolyn, the little voice answered.

"Right." Lindsey nodded. Carolyn would be crushed. But better Carolyn than Lindsey.

Lindsey threw back her covers and slipped out of bed. She tiptoed over to the mirror and stood before it. Then she whispered the chant.

She waited. But nothing happened. She didn't see anything in the mirror but her own reflection.

Lindsey made her wish anyway. "Bloody Mary, if you are real, I wish I'd get the lead in the play. I would give anything for that."

Lindsey waited for another minute before she

turned away from the mirror and got back into bed. Even Bloody Mary wasn't going to help her.

But Lindsey never saw the face looking out at her while she slept. It was smiling, but the smile was not a kind one. It was evil.

14

The bed covers flew off Lindsey's body, startling her awake.

It was only then that she heard the ear-splitting noise coming from the table beside her.

"Lindsey!" Her mother shouted to be heard over the obnoxious buzzing of her alarm clock.

Lindsey's eyes were still blurry as she looked up to see her mother standing beside the bed, her hands on her hips.

"How could you possibly sleep through this alarm?" Mrs. Jordan asked as she reached to turn it off.

Finally there was quiet. Lindsey wished it could

stay that way. She was so tired, she wished she could just pull her covers back up around her and go back to sleep.

But her mother wasn't about to let that happen. "You'd better get up, young lady. You're going to be late for school."

Who cares? Lindsey thought. The last thing in the world she wanted to do was go to school and face Carolyn Berger.

"Let's get a move on it," her mother said, refusing to move herself until she saw Lindsey get out of that bed.

Lindsey's legs felt as though they had hundred-pound weights attached to them as she swung them over the side of the bed and sat up.

"Why are you so sleepy this morning?" her mother asked, sounding genuinely concerned. She reached out to touch Lindsey's forehead. "You're not coming down with anything, are you?"

"I'm okay," Lindsey assured her. "I didn't get much sleep last night. I was too nervous because the cast list for the play is going to be posted this morning. I'm sure Carolyn's going to get the lead."

"You don't know that," her mother told her, trying to sound encouraging.

Yes, I do, Lindsey thought. There was only one hope, and it was a long shot. "Hey, Mom," Lindsey started. "What do you know about Bloody Mary?"

"Which one?" her mother asked.

Which one? Lindsey thought. *How many Bloody Marys do you know?* "The one in the mirror," Lindsey answered tentatively.

"Oh." Her mother chuckled. "*That* Bloody Mary."

"Yeah," Lindsey said. "*That* Bloody Mary."

"Well, I can tell you that you and your friends did not invent the game," her mother informed her. "Kids have been playing Bloody Mary for as long as I can remember—or at least some version of the game," she explained. "It depends upon where you grow up."

"What do you mean?" Lindsey asked.

"Well, when I was a kid, we didn't call the game Bloody Mary. We called it 'Mary, Mary.' And I grew up in Connecticut," her mother reminded her. "We didn't chant, either. We just lit a candle in front of the mirror and said 'Mary, Mary' thirteen times. My cousin, Lillian, called the game 'Mary Worth,'" she continued. "She grew up in Virginia. And your Aunt Maggie called the game 'Mary Billingsworth,' and she grew up around here. No matter where you come from, there always seems to be a game with a scary Mary in the mirror."

"Did you ever see a scary Mary?" Lindsey wanted to know.

"All the time," her mother replied, sounding very serious about it.

"Really?" Lindsey gasped.

Her mother laughed. "Of course not," she answered. "I was teasing you, Linds. It's just a game."

"I know," Lindsey lied. "I just wondered how it started, that's all."

"I'm not so sure about that," her mother said. She started walking around the room, straightening up as she continued to talk. "Some of the kids in my neighborhood thought that Mary was a good spirit, kind of like Aladdin's genie, only trapped in a mirror instead of a lamp. But some of the kids insisted that Mary was a witch who preyed upon the innocent wishes of children so she could continue to do her evil bidding right here on earth."

"What did you think?" Lindsey wanted to know.

"I thought the whole thing was nonsense," her mother declared, stopping in front of the mirror. "Good or bad," she continued, studying herself for a moment, "there's no such thing as wish-granting spirits."

Then suddenly she let out a panicked scream.

15

Lindsey jumped off her bed and rushed to her mother's side as Mrs. Jordan continued to peer into the glass, looking horrified. "What is it?" Lindsey asked nervously. "Is Bloody Mary in there?"

"Bloody Mary?" Mrs. Jordan chuckled, glancing at her daughter. "I wish. Maybe she could get rid of this gray hair."

Lindsey let out a sigh as her mother pointed out the source of her angst. It was one piece of hair shining through the rest of the chestnut strands on the top of her head.

"I'm way too young for this," Mrs. Jordan groaned, tugging the silvery strand from her head.

"Ouch." Lindsey reacted as if her mother had just pulled a piece of Lindsey's own hair out. "Doesn't that hurt?"

"Not as much as my ego," her mother joked.

Lindsey smiled. "So what are you going to do if the rest of them turn gray—pull them all out?"

"Who knows," her mother said. "Maybe I'll dye them all purple."

"Green might look better on you," Lindsey told her.

Mrs. Jordan laughed as she turned from the mirror. "You'd better get going," she said. "Otherwise, you won't have time for breakfast."

"I don't want breakfast," Lindsey told her mother. "I'll just throw it up."

Mrs. Jordan smiled sympathetically. "You know what?" she said. "No matter what happens today, I'm still going to be proud of you. And you should be, too—part, or no part. Besides, what's that old show-business saying?"

Lindsey shrugged. She didn't know any old show-business sayings.

"Oh, yeah." Her mother finally remembered. "There's no such thing as small parts, only small actors," she said. "The point is, Lindsey, participating is what's really important."

Lindsey rolled her eyes. "Tell that to Carolyn."

Her mother grinned. "Either way, Linds, it's not the end of the world."

Less than an hour later, it certainly felt that way.

In fact, Lindsey wanted to crawl into a hole and hide the moment she saw the cast list. It was pinned up on the bulletin board outside the auditorium for all the school to read. Luckily, she and Bree had gotten to school even later than usual, so the hallway was already empty.

"How can this be?" Bree gasped, staring in horror at the name listed next to the lead.

But seeing Carolyn Berger's name typed in bold letters next to the lead was nowhere near as traumatizing to Lindsey as what was typed next to it in parentheses:

Lindsey Jordan—understudy.

"I'm never going to live this down," Lindsey said, trying to hold back the tears.

"You are, too," Bree said. "It's just a stupid play. And everybody knows you should have gotten that part. I can't believe what a jerk Mr. Kreeger is."

Lindsey knew that Bree was trying to make her feel better, but there was nothing anyone could say or do to stop the anger, hurt, and embarrassment Lindsey was feeling. She just wanted to disappear.

"Let's get out of here before anybody sees us," Lindsey said. "The last thing I need now is for Carolyn and Nancy to be laughing in my face."

"Don't worry," Bree said as they headed for their classroom, "Ralphie will take care of them."

Ralphie said as much, too, the moment Lindsey and Bree got to class, two seconds before the bell rang.

All through the morning, Lindsey's three friends tried to cheer her up. They whispered mean things about Carolyn and passed around pictures they'd drawn of Nancy Patanski splitting her pants. But Lindsey wasn't laughing. The fact was that Nancy Patanski was right— Lindsey was a loser.

The moment the lunch bell rang, Lindsey told her

friends to go on without her. Then she went to the nurse's office complaining of a stomachache so she could avoid going to the cafeteria and facing Carolyn and Nancy.

The school nurse was great when it came to stomachaches. She let you lie down for as long as you wanted, and she didn't call your mother unless you had a fever.

So when Lindsey's temperature came out normal, the nurse let Lindsey crawl into a ball on the cot in her office and let her stay there until the three o'clock bell rang.

The moment Lindsey hit the hall, she started to run. She didn't even bother to go to her locker. She ran straight for the exit. All she wanted to do was get out of there so she could be alone with her disappointment.

Luckily, Lindsey wouldn't have to face anyone until Tuesday morning. Thanks to teacher conferences, she'd have three whole days to try to pull herself together. She was sure she'd need them, too, because the next six weeks of her life were going to be torture. Every day would be filled with humiliation as Carolyn walked around school acting like a star while Nancy Patanski treated Lindsey like a loser.

And then the night of the play would come. Carolyn would have center stage to take her bows. She would get a standing ovation. Whether the play was good or bad, the star always got a standing ovation. Lindsey didn't know how she could cope with Carolyn getting all the glory—the glory that should have been hers.

When Lindsey arrived home, she let herself go. Angry sobs escaped her throat as she ran up the steps onto the porch.

She opened the door quietly, hoping to sneak past her mother to her room. She wasn't ready to tell her what had happened. Her mother would try to comfort her, and Lindsey didn't want comfort. There was no comfort in this.

Luckily, Mrs. Jordan was in the kitchen with Alyssa, scolding her for not taking care of the puppy. Lindsey made it into her room unnoticed. She closed the door, leaned against it, and cried some more.

Images of Carolyn and Nancy mocking her filled her head until she felt as though it was going to explode.

Then an even worse thought occurred to her. As Carolyn's understudy, she would have to go to rehearsals every day, standing on the stage in the background while Carolyn commanded all the attention. She couldn't turn down her role as understudy. Not only would she look like a loser, she'd look like a *sore* loser.

Lindsey took a step toward her bed. She was about to throw herself down onto it, but she stopped when she caught sight of herself in the mirror. She walked toward it, looking at her reflection.

When she was nearly right up against the mirror, she stopped and stared into her eyes, watching the tears well up in them. Instead of blinking or spilling the tears, she tilted her head and felt the tears wash across her eyes. They pooled up in the corners, still not spilling. It was an odd sensation. She did it again, tilting her head the other way.

As she concentrated on tilting her head and staring at her eyes, her image in the mirror began to blur.

Finally, Lindsey blinked hard, and the tears spilled down her face. She wiped at her eyes to dry them.

But when she looked back into the mirror, she realized it wasn't her vision that was blurred. It was the mirror itself that had fogged over. It looked like the inside of a car windshield on a cold day.

Lindsey could actually see the condensation. She put her hand to the glass. It was wet. She wiped it with her hand. Then she stepped back, startled by what she saw.

The image behind the fog was not her own anymore. It was Carolyn's.

Lindsey stood there, stunned. What was she seeing?

It was like watching a movie without sound. And Carolyn was the star.

Carolyn was standing outside the school building with Nancy Patanski beside her. There were other kids there, too. And they all looked like they were congratulating Carolyn. Suddenly, Carolyn dropped all her books and grabbed her stomach, as if she'd been shot. Within seconds, she fell to her knees, screaming and crying in pain.

Beside her, Nancy Patanski was screaming as well.

Lindsey couldn't hear what she was saying, but it looked like she was calling out for help.

Lindsey took a step back from the mirror, terrified.

Suddenly, it was as if Carolyn were looking directly at Lindsey, as if Lindsey could save her.

But Lindsey watched helplessly as Carolyn toppled down the steps and collapsed to the ground.

Then the image disappeared.

Lindsey watched in horror as blood began to trickle down the shimmering surface of the mirror.

16

This isn't real! Lindsey's brain was screaming inside her head as she stood watching the trickle of blood roll down the glass.

Her body trembled uncontrollably as she reached out to touch the mirror. She needed to prove to herself that it was all an illusion, just her imagination. But the moment her fingers touched the glass, Lindsey pulled her hand back in horror.

Her fingers were covered with blood!

Lindsey opened her mouth to scream, but the terror was strangling her, and no sound came out.

A knock at the door made Lindsey jump as it forced the scream from her throat.

Mrs. Jordan pushed the door open quickly. "Lindsey, what's wrong?" she asked.

Lindsey held out her hand as if to show her mother. But when she looked down at it, it was perfectly clean. She spun toward the mirror, but all she saw was her own reflection.

"What's wrong?" Mrs. Jordan repeated.

Lindsey couldn't possibly tell her mother what she'd just seen. She'd sound like a nutcase. Her mother would never believe her. She would think Lindsey was imagining things.

Maybe she was. Maybe she was losing her mind.

One way or another, she had to find out.

"Nothing's wrong, Mom," Lindsey lied, trying to keep her voice from trembling the way her body still was. "You scared me, that's all."

Her mother bought the excuse. "So how did you make out at school today?" she asked. "Did you get the part that you wanted?"

Lindsey shook her head.

"Aw, Linds," Mrs. Jordan said as she wrapped her arms around her daughter. "I'm sorry. You must be so disappointed."

"Not really," Lindsey lied again. She had no time to be crying on her mother's shoulder. Not now. She had to get back to school. "Mr. Kreeger made me the understudy," she said. "And that's almost as good. In fact, I'm going to run back to school and pick up the script now if that's okay? Mr. Kreeger said they'd be ready by four o'clock."

"Sure, Linds," her mother said, looking proud of her.

It made Lindsey feel worse than she already did. She hated lying to her mother, but she didn't have a choice.

"Just be home by five," her mother told her.

"I will," Lindsey said. She kissed her mother goodbye and raced for the door.

Lindsey didn't stop running until she hit the circular drive in front of the school building.

There was a crowd gathered on the front steps— right where she had seen Carolyn fall in the mirror.

She could see Mr. Steele and a group of teachers trying to break it up.

Lindsey's heart was beating so hard and so fast, she could barely catch her breath. The image in the mirror was real! Something terrible had happened to Carolyn Berger. Lindsey was sure of it.

She wanted to move closer, but her feet wouldn't let her. She was too afraid she'd see Carolyn lying on the steps, screaming in agony, crying for help. There was no way she could face that. Not again, not for real.

Luckily, she didn't have to.

"Lindsey!" Bree's voice suddenly pulled Lindsey out of the dizzy spin her head was in. Bree was running down the drive toward her, with Ralphie and Tommy right on her heels.

"You're never going to believe what just happened," Tommy announced, all out of breath.

"Well, it didn't *just* happen," Bree said. "It happened like twenty minutes ago."

Lindsey's legs suddenly felt as if they were turning to jelly.

"Carolyn Berger collapsed right on the front steps,"

Tommy told her. "There were cop cars and an ambulance and everything."

"Yeah," Bree said. "Everybody thought she was dead."

Lindsey's stomach raced to her throat. If she didn't pass out first, she was sure to throw up.

"But the ambulance workers woke her up," Ralphie continued. "They think her appendix exploded, or something."

"Is she going to be okay?" Lindsey could barely choke out the words.

"The ambulance guy said she'd be fine," Bree answered. "But she's probably going to need an operation. And she's going to be in the hospital for at least a week."

"Then she's going to be out of school for a couple weeks more," Tommy added.

"This just can't be happening." Lindsey's thoughts escaped in a whimper.

"What can't be happening?" Bree asked.

"This," Lindsey said. "Carolyn just can't be sick."

"Well, she is," Ralphie blurted.

"It's not your fault, Linds," Tommy said, reacting to how upset Lindsey was becoming.

"Yes, it is," Lindsey admitted. "It's all my fault."

Ralphie's face immediately lost all its color. And Bree grabbed her stomach as if her own appendix were about to erupt.

"How is this your fault?" Tommy still wasn't getting it—at least not for another second. Then his face turned as terrified as Bree's.

"Lindsey, you didn't!" Bree gasped.

Lindsey just nodded.

"Oh, man." Ralphie cringed. "Bloody Mary made Carolyn's appendix explode!"

Lindsey looked at Tommy, hoping he would say something that would convince her this was a coincidence, too. But Tommy stood silent—and terrified.

"You did this today?" Bree asked, sounding appalled.

"No," Lindsey said. "I did it last night. And I was sure it didn't work when I saw the cast list this morning. So I didn't even tell you guys about it."

"We made a deal, Lindsey." Bree sounded as upset

as Lindsey felt. "We weren't supposed to make any more wishes."

"I know." Lindsey's voice was full of regret. "I just wanted that stupid part."

"Well, now you've got it," Ralphie said.

"And now I don't want it," Lindsey cried. "I don't want it at all."

"Tell that to Bloody Mary," Ralphie said.

17

Lindsey was very quiet at dinner that evening. As her family discussed the day, she barely listened. All she could think about was Bloody Mary.

When the puppy pawed her leg, begging for food, she pushed him away. He was just another terrible reminder of what their wishes were doing to other people.

"What's with you tonight, Linds?" her father asked.

"Nothing," she lied. She didn't know how to begin to explain to them.

"Does it have something to do with the play?" her mother pressed.

Lindsey shook her head—another lie. She had explained to her parents everything that had happened—excluding the part about Bloody Mary and the mirror—as they were setting the table for dinner.

"What happened to Carolyn is very sad, but it's not your fault," her mother told her sympathetically.

Lindsey almost began to cry. She wanted to confess that it *was* her fault. But she knew she would only sound crazy, and that her parents would never believe her.

"Well, now seems like the perfect time for my good news," her father said, changing the subject.

"What good news?" Mrs. Jordan asked, trying to sound as if she didn't already know.

"What is it, Daddy?" Alyssa asked, sounding a whole lot like their mother.

Lindsey felt as though she was the only one who didn't have a clue.

"Where's the one place in the world you guys have always wanted to go?" Mr. Jordan asked, smiling.

Lindsey shrugged.

"I don't know," Alyssa answered slyly.

"Disney World?" Mrs. Jordan directed the question toward her children.

"You're kidding," Lindsey gasped.

"We're going to Disney World!" Alyssa exclaimed. But it seemed as if she'd known it all along.

"That's right," Mr. Jordan said happily. "We're leaving the day after school lets out. And we're staying a week."

"I can't believe it," Lindsey said. For a moment, she began to cheer up.

But only for a moment.

Lindsey's happiness was shattered when Alyssa leaned over and whispered in her ear, "I made a wish to Bloody Mary."

18

W e can't go to Disney World," Lindsey announced. "We just can't."

"What on earth are you talking about?" her mother asked, surprised.

"I thought it was something you've always wanted to do," her father said. "I thought this would make you happy."

"Are you crazy?" Alyssa added her two cents.

"You don't understand," Lindsey said. "If we go on this trip, something bad is sure to happen."

"Lindsey, you're being silly," her mother told her. "What makes you think something bad will happen?"

Lindsey had no choice but to explain. She told her parents all about Bloody Mary. She told them about the puppy lady, Mrs. Wickley, Nancy, and Carolyn.

They listened, but Lindsey could tell that they didn't believe a word she was saying. And they certainly were not about to cancel their trip just because Alyssa admitted to having wished for it.

"We all wish for things," her mother said. "And some of the time our wishes come true."

"But you don't wish to Bloody Mary," Lindsey argued.

"Bloody Mary had nothing to do with anything that's happened," her father assured her.

But he was wrong. Lindsey knew it. What she didn't know was how to convince them. "You just don't understand," she started.

The doorbell interrupted her.

"Why don't you go get that?" Mrs. Jordan asked Lindsey.

She suspected it was because her mother wanted to get her out of the room so that she and Lindsey's father could talk about her. *Fine,* she thought, getting up to go answer the door.

When she opened the front door, she found Tommy, Ralphie, and Bree waiting on the porch.

"You're never going to believe what we found out," Bree declared before anybody else had a chance to say anything. "After you went home this afternoon, we all went back to Ralphie's house to see what we could find out about Bloody Mary," she told Lindsey.

"And we found out a lot," Tommy added.

"But *not* from Ralphie's computer, like we thought we would," Bree explained. "From Ralphie's mom. Tell her, Ralphie." She elbowed him to get him talking.

"There really was a Bloody Mary," Ralphie told Lindsey ominously. "Only her real name was Mary Billingsworth."

The moment Lindsey heard the name, she recognized it. "That's the name my Aunt Maggie used to call Bloody Mary," she informed them, stepping onto the porch and closing the door behind her. "My Aunt Maggie grew up around here."

"So did Ralphie's mom," Bree told her.

"And so did Mary Billingsworth," Ralphie announced.

Lindsey gasped.

"She lived in this town like a hundred and fifty years ago," Ralphie told her.

"And she was a witch!" Bree exclaimed. "A really, really bad witch. She used to steal little kids so that she could suck the life out of them. Huh, Ralphie?"

Ralphie nodded.

"Your mom told you that?" Lindsey wanted to know.

Ralphie nodded, but Bree answered. "Yeah. While Tommy and I were on Ralphie's computer, Ralphie went downstairs to ask his mother to get us a pizza and she ended up telling him about Bloody Mary."

"What else did she say?" Lindsey asked.

"She said that Bloody Mary had a sister named Beatrice Billingsworth," Ralphie went on. "And Beatrice ended up in a nuthouse because of Mary."

"How come?" Lindsey wanted to know.

"Mary kept trying to concoct evil spells that would let her live forever, which was why she kept stealing kids," Ralphie explained. "She needed their souls or something. But she got old and sick anyway. And she was about to die."

"Beatrice was taking care of her," Bree interrupted.

"Right," Ralphie confirmed. "The night Bloody Mary was lying in bed about to die, Beatrice left the room for just a minute, to get medicine or something. When she came back, Mary was gone."

"Completely gone!" Bree punctuated the point.

"It was as though she'd dissolved into thin air," Ralphie proclaimed. "Beatrice looked all around the room, but she couldn't find Mary anywhere. Until she turned and looked into the mirror."

"Mary Billingsworth was inside the mirror!" Bree stole Ralphie's thunder.

"That was why Beatrice ended up in the nuthouse, until she was like ninety-nine years old," Ralphie went on. "Because nobody believed her."

"I believe her," Lindsey said.

"Me, too," Bree agreed. "Think of how the chant goes." She recited the last two lines.

In return for what you give,
We will let your spirit live.

Everyone fell silent for a moment.

"Look," Tommy said, sounding unnerved. "We don't know any of this for sure. We couldn't find any information about Mary Billingsworth online," he reminded Ralphie.

"Yeah," Bree agreed. "But when we looked up 'Bloody Mary,' we didn't find out anything for sure, either," she told Lindsey. "The name 'Bloody Mary' can refer to anybody with blood on their hands. So there are lots of 'Bloody Marys' out there. And lots of 'Bloody Mary' games."

Lindsey shuddered at the thought.

"So if there are lots of Bloody Marys, and lots of Bloody Mary games, how come nobody else has ever seen her?" Tommy posed the question.

"Nobody but us," Bree corrected him.

"It's simple," Ralphie said. "None of us ever saw Bloody Mary until your mom brought home that antique mirror. You know what I think?"

Ralphie didn't have to tell her. Lindsey was already thinking the same thing.

But Ralphie said it out loud anyway. "The mirror that's in your bedroom now was the mirror that belonged to Mary Billingsworth. It's the mirror that she got sucked into when she died."

19

Ralphie was right. Lindsey was sure of it. After all, it wasn't until the "valuable antique" arrived at the house that Bloody Mary invaded their lives.

"You've got to get that mirror out of your house," Ralphie said, which was exactly what Lindsey was thinking.

But that was easier said than done.

"There's no way my mom's going to get rid of that mirror," Lindsey told them. "She thinks it's the greatest thing on earth."

"What if you tell her that Bloody Mary lives in it?" Bree asked. "And that she's not very nice."

"I did," Lindsey said. "I even told her what she did to Mrs. Wickley and Carolyn and Nancy and the old lady. But she wouldn't believe a word of it."

"Then you've at least got to get that thing out of your room," Tommy told her.

"Why?" Lindsey cried. "It's not going to change anything. Bloody Mary will still be in my house. And Alyssa will still be wishing up a storm," she informed them.

"Alyssa's making more wishes?" Bree asked, alarmed.

Lindsey nodded. "Guess who's going to Disney World?"

"No, sir!" Ralphie gasped.

"Yes, sir," Lindsey said. "Thanks to Bloody Mary, my parents are taking us to Florida the first week of summer vacation."

"Oh, man!" Ralphie cringed. "No way you can go to Disney World. Bloody Mary might try to kill Mickey Mouse or something."

"Who cares about Mickey Mouse!" Bree backhanded Ralphie. "What if she tries to do something bad to Lindsey?"

Everyone swallowed hard.

"Wait a minute," Bree exclaimed. "Why don't we go inside and tell your mom what Ralphie's mom said? Or maybe we should make Ralphie's mom call her."

Lindsey thought about it for a second. Maybe if her mother heard about Bloody Mary from another adult, she'd take her more seriously.

"Does your mom know what's going on now?" Lindsey asked Ralphie.

"Not really," Ralphie answered. "Besides, I don't think she'd believe us."

"Why not?" Bree snapped. "She just told you that Mary Billingsworth was real."

"Yeah," Ralphie shot back. "A hundred and fifty years ago, not right this minute. She told me how the game got started, that's all. She never said she believed that it worked."

Lindsey sighed. "Well, does she at least have any proof that Mary Billingsworth existed a hundred and fifty years ago?"

Ralphie shook his head. "Not really," he said. "All she knows is what her cousin told her when they were kids."

"Did it occur to you that maybe her cousin made it up?" Tommy huffed.

Ralphie looked crushed.

"Terrific," Bree groaned. "Now we don't know anything more than we did this afternoon."

"Yes, we do," Lindsey said. "I believe Ralphie's mother. That mirror has to be Mary Billingsworth's. It's the only thing that makes sense. We've just got to figure out a way to prove it. Then maybe I can convince my mom to get rid of the mirror for good."

"And how are we supposed to get proof?" Bree asked.

That was a good question. Unfortunately, Lindsey didn't have an answer.

"Wait a minute," Tommy said a moment later. "If Mary Billingsworth really lived in this town more than a hundred years ago, then she's probably buried in that cemetery behind the old firehouse. Or, if she disappeared, then at least her sister, Beatrice, should be there."

"You mean Camp Graveyard-Buried-Bats?" Ralphie asked.

Tommy nodded. "Yup. That's the only place she'd be."

Camp Graveyard-Buried-Bats was the name Ralphie had given to the day camp they all attended before kindergarten. It wasn't really a camp; it was arts and crafts at the firehouse, with playtime in the parking lot behind it. The parking lot was right next to a two-hundred-year-old cemetery, and even though it was surrounded by a wrought-iron fence, Ralphie was terrified of it.

In fact, his mom had had to drag him out of the car every morning, kicking and screaming. When she managed to get him inside the building, he wouldn't come out again. Not until the day the camp counselors found bats in the basement.

That was the day Ralphie climbed onto the roof, and the firefighters had to get him down.

Ralphie still refused to step within sixty feet of that cemetery.

"Forget it, Tommy," Ralphie said. "I know what you're thinking. There's no way I'm going."

"Oh, come on, Ralphie," Tommy protested. "We have to go to the cemetery. It's the only way to get proof that Mary and Beatrice Billingsworth really existed."

"I don't need any proof," Ralphie said. "I believe it already!"

"Yeah?" Bree barked. "Well, if you don't go, and Mary Billingsworth really does try to kill Mickey Mouse, then you can just blame yourself. Because if Lindsey doesn't find a way to convince her mom that that mirror is trouble, it's going to happen."

Bree's reasoning sounded so ridiculous, even Lindsey had to laugh. But somehow it worked.

"Fine," Ralphie growled. "But you just better hope that some other spook doesn't follow us home from that cemetery. And I'm telling you now, the minute I see a bat, I'm out of there."

They finally had a plan—and a tiny bit of hope.

Lindsey ran back inside to tell her parents that they were going for a walk. She didn't tell them where she was going, but she promised to be back before nine. As she headed outside again, she grabbed a flashlight from the garage.

It wasn't until they'd walked fifteen minutes and crossed over Cedar Lane that Ralphie started to freak. Camp Graveyard-Buried-Bats was half a block away.

"This is stupid." Ralphie started to ramble. "Even if we prove to Lindsey's mom that there really was a Mary Billingsworth, there's no way to be sure Lindsey's mom will get rid of the mirror. And even if she does, how do we know that Mary Billingsworth will leave us alone? After all, she followed us to school, remember?"

Lindsey was worried about that herself.

"That's not going to happen," Tommy assured her. "Once that mirror is out of our lives, Bloody Mary will be, too."

Lindsey hoped that was true as they walked past the old firehouse and into the parking lot.

Lindsey turned on her flashlight.

The firehouse had been closed for years. The city council had planned to rebuild it, but the mayor had decided to construct a new one across town. As a result, the old firehouse was deserted and had started to crumble. It was more than a little bit creepy.

So were the parking lot and the short gravel drive that led to the rusted gates of the old cemetery.

"I don't want to do this," Ralphie cried as they reached the gates.

Lindsey wasn't so sure she wanted to do it, either. The cemetery had never bothered her when she was a kid, but now, in the pitch darkness, and with all that was happening, she was beginning to think they might be in for real trouble.

Tommy pushed on the gate. It wouldn't budge.

"Darn it," Ralphie said, barely containing the excitement in his voice. "They must have closed it for the night. I guess we'll have to check back tomorrow." Ralphie spun around to leave, but Bree grabbed his arm.

"We're not leaving," she told him. "Not until we get in there and see."

Tommy pushed on the gate again. It still wouldn't move.

Then Lindsey gave it a try.

Then Bree.

Then Tommy, Lindsey, and Bree all together.

"We're not getting in," Ralphie said, sounding relieved. "See?"

"Oh, yes, we are," Tommy insisted. "We'll just have to climb over the gate."

"Are you nuts?" Ralphie snapped. "I'm not breaking into a cemetery! It's quite clear that the dead people don't want us in there!"

Just then, it became perfectly clear that somebody did. Suddenly, the rusted old gate started to creak open by itself.

20

Every muscle in Lindsey's body tightened with terror as she watched the gate swing open. It was almost as if someone or something inside the cemetery was pulling the gate. Lindsey half expected that at any moment she'd see a worm-eaten, fleshless zombie face welcoming them to the home of the dead.

Ralphie must have been thinking the very same thing, because he spun around fast, ready to run. But before he'd taken even one step, a strange, howling wind blew up from behind them, knocking Ralphie onto his butt.

The wind was fierce, and colder than death. As it

slammed into Lindsey's back, she had to fight to stay on her feet. It started pushing her with a vengeance, straight through the gate.

"*Aaaaaaghhhhhh!*" Ralphie wailed along with the wind as he scrambled to get up. "What the heck is going on?"

Beyond the gate, in the graveyard, the air was calm. Leafy tree branches at the far end of the cemetery were still. But behind them, along the drive, the trees were bending and blowing with such force, they looked as if they would snap in two.

Tommy and Bree were being shoved through the gate as well, with Ralphie hanging around Tommy's neck, screaming.

Then, as the wind pushed past them and into the graveyard, it died as suddenly as it had started up.

Tommy finally managed to pry Ralphie's arms from his neck, and everyone's heart started beating again.

"That wasn't wind!" Ralphie cried. "That was some spook swirling back to its grave!"

Lindsey hated to admit it, but that's what she thought, too. Especially since the gate had swung open even before the wind whirled by. But she wasn't about to point that out now, at least not to Ralphie. It would only make things worse.

"I say we just get this over with," Lindsey told them, trying to sound brave. Then she took a deep breath and stepped forward.

Tommy followed, with Bree hanging on to his shirt.

"Are you coming?" Lindsey asked, shining the beam of her flashlight in Ralphie's terrified face.

"Not in this lifetime," Ralphie shot back.

"Fine," Tommy retorted. "Then you'll just have to wait here, all by yourself."

A moment later, Ralphie was glued to their sides.

As Lindsey headed for the first row of worn-down tombstones, the ground beneath her feet felt strange. It seemed soft, like quicksand. She couldn't help thinking that she'd be sucked right into a grave.

She tried to convince herself that her imagination was just overactive. The ground inside the cemetery was the same as the ground on the outside. But it was hard to believe that, especially when the turf under her feet felt so . . . different.

"Barnabus Davenport." Tommy read the name on the very first tombstone. "Born 1812. Died 1862."

"Who cares?" Bree said nervously. "Just keep moving, will you? I can't stand stepping on dead people. It gives me the creeps."

Lindsey hurried on, as Ralphie started doing what looked like a Mexican hat dance. He was hopping up and down so fast, his feet barely touched the ground.

"Elizabeth Davenport," Bree quickly read as the flashlight illuminated the next stone. The next, "Bartholomew Davenport."

"Looks like this whole row is Davenports," Tommy commented as they moved even faster.

The next row was Fredricksons—Samuel, James, Helen, and Richard.

Next to them were the Hadleys and the Monroes.

Ralphie made sure to apologize to all of the dead people as he danced over their graves.

"It's starting to look like Ralphie's mom was wrong," Tommy said as they finally approached the lopsided stones in the last row, at the back of the cemetery.

Lindsey was beginning to think so, too, until the light from her flashlight caught an enormous carved *B* on the very first stone.

This was it. Although the rest of the letters were covered with grime, Lindsey was sure of it.

For a moment, everyone but Ralphie, who continued to hop from one foot to the other, stood frozen. Then Tommy finally got up the nerve to wipe the filth from the stone with the sleeve of his sweatshirt. One by one, the rest of the letters came clear.

Lindsey's heart skipped six whole beats as she stared at the name before her. "They're here," she cried. "The Billingsworths are here!"

"Did your mom say anything about Lucretia Billingsworth?" Tommy asked, reading the first name.

Ralphie shook his head.

"What about Ezra?" Bree gulped as they slowly moved down the line.

Again Ralphie shook his head.

Lindsey held her breath as they passed three more stones marking the bodies of Barnaby, Cornelius, and

Edwin. With each passing grave, she was becoming more and more frightened. What if they really did find Mary Billingsworth? Worse still, what if they didn't?

There were only two more stones left. As Lindsey shined the flashlight at the first one, Ralphie gasped loudly. It wasn't Mary, but it was definitely a name they all recognized.

"I told you my mom wasn't lying!" Ralphie declared. "We're standing on top of Beatrice Billingsworth, Bloody Mary's sister!"

Bree caught her breath, as if ready to panic. Tommy was standing as stiff as Beatrice's stone, looking as pale as a ghost.

Lindsey's whole body started to shake. "Beatrice Billingsworth." Her voice trembled as she read the name and the dates. "Born 1812. Died 1911."

"I told you she was in a nuthouse until she was ninety-nine years old!" Ralphie blurted. "And if Beatrice Billingsworth was real, then Mary was, too!"

Lindsey's eyes moved to the very last stone. It wasn't gray like the others. It was jet black and shaped like a heart. And it wasn't standing up. It was lying facedown in the dirt, covered with maggots and slugs.

"We've got to lift it," she told Tommy. "We have to see whose it is."

"Are you nuts?" Tommy shot back. "I'm not touching that thing. It's crawling with slugs."

"Please," Lindsey begged. "I have to see. I have to know for sure."

Tommy cringed, but he found a fallen tree limb on the other side of the cemetery fence. He pulled the branch through the rusted iron bars and stuck the tip of the branch under the edge of the black, chiseled stone. And as he pried up the stone and flipped it over, Lindsey almost threw up.

Black, slimy snakes slithered right out of the grave, covering the ground where the stone had been lying.

"Snakes!" Ralphie screamed. "Get me out of here!"

He took off like a shot, with Bree right behind him.

Tommy and Lindsey stood frozen, staring in horror at the name that was now facing upward.

Mary Billingsworth was real.

"Lindsey, look," Tommy exclaimed, pointing to the dates under the name. "Guess who's not dead!"

Lindsey blinked hard. The only date she could see was 1802, the year Mary Billingsworth was born. The death date was blank.

"If she's not in her grave, where is she?" Lindsey cried.

But the answer was clear . . . as clear as the reflection in Lindsey's bedroom mirror.

21

I want that mirror out of this house!" Lindsey told her parents.

After their trip to the cemetery she'd gone right back home to report what they'd seen, but she couldn't make her parents believe her.

Lindsey's mother and father looked at each other, exasperated. She knew they'd had it with her. They were about to blow a fuse.

Still, her father's voice was calm when he said, "Linds, you're being silly about this. You and your friends have gotten yourselves all worked up over an old story."

Lindsey wasn't about to give up. "It's not just a story," she insisted. "Mary Billingsworth is real. My friends don't even want to come inside this house anymore," she went on. "Not until that mirror is gone."

"I'm not getting rid of it," her mother said. "It's a beautiful work of art. If you don't appreciate it, we'll move it into Alyssa's room."

"That's a great idea!" Alyssa exclaimed.

"That's a terrible idea!" Lindsey shouted at her mother. "Don't you understand what that little urchin will do if you put the mirror in her room? She'll be calling up Bloody Mary every two seconds. Then we'll be in big, big trouble."

"I'm not an urchin," Alyssa growled, sticking her tongue out at Lindsey.

"That's right," Lindsey snapped. "You're a greedy, stupid little brat."

"Mommy!" Alyssa cried.

"Lindsey," her mother scolded. "That's enough. I will not have you talking to your sister like that. You apologize right this minute."

Lindsey was so frustrated she was practically in tears.

"You don't understand," she shrieked. "If we don't get rid of that mirror, something really terrible will happen!"

Lindsey's mother just glared at her.

"If you don't apologize to your sister, something terrible *is* sure to happen," her father warned.

Alyssa smirked.

"Forget it!" Lindsey said. She ran out of the kitchen and down the hallway into the foyer.

"You get back here right now, young lady," her mother called after her.

Lindsey wasn't about to turn back. She couldn't deal with them for one more second. She needed some time alone—to pull herself together, to find a way to get them to see what was happening.

Lindsey grabbed the stair rail and took the first step. She would go to her bedroom and lock herself in, the way she always did when she needed a time-out.

"Lindsey!" her mother called. She was following.

Lindsey didn't answer. She just moved up the stairs even faster. It wasn't until she'd reached the top that she realized she couldn't go to her bedroom. The mirror was there.

She headed for the bathroom instead.

She could hear her parents coming up the stairs, with Alyssa right behind them, just as she ducked inside the bathroom.

Within seconds, her mother was pounding on the door. "Lindsey, you come out here right now!"

Her father's voice was a little more gentle, but no less insistent. "Open the door, Lindsey," he commanded.

"You're going to get it," Alyssa gloated.

Lindsey felt as though her head was about to explode.

"I wish you would all just leave me alone," she cried, leaning against the bathroom door.

A sparkle of light caught her eye.

It was coming from the mirror that covered the wall above the sink.

Lindsey put her hand to her mouth, as if she could force the words back in.

But it was too late now. She'd made her wish.

22

N o!" Lindsey screamed the instant she realized her mistake.

But her voice was drowned out by a louder noise coming from outside the bathroom. It was a terrible howling.

Lindsey unlocked the door and turned the knob to open it.

The door wouldn't budge.

She put her full weight into it and pulled with all her might. It was as if the door had been nailed shut.

The noise outside grew louder and louder. It sounded

as though there was a tornado moving through the hallway.

"Mommy!" Lindsey screamed as she tugged franti-
cally at the door. "Daddy!"

She was answered by the sounds of her parents'
cries, and Alyssa's. "Help! Somebody help us!"

The wind was wailing furiously. It rattled the door
so hard Lindsey was sure it would fly off its hinges. But
the door held fast.

Lindsey was trapped inside, knowing that outside,
something terrible was happening to her family.

What have I done? she thought, glancing back at the
mirror.

Her own reflection began to fade as another image
took shape. It was the hallway right outside the door.

Lindsey couldn't believe her eyes. There was a tornado out there. But something about it was unusual.
This tornado wasn't standing upright, the way she'd
always seen them in pictures. This tornado was swirling on its side. And it was coming from her room.

Lindsey saw her parents and Alyssa sprawled on the
floor just outside the door. The wind was whipping at

them furiously. And they were hanging on to one another, grabbing desperately at the walls and the carpet, trying to avoid being sucked into the swirling black funnel.

"No!" Lindsey screamed again as the tornado inched closer. "Don't take them. I don't wish my family would leave me alone. I wish they *wouldn't* leave me alone!"

Lindsey heard their pitiful cries as she saw the tornado begin to devour them, dragging them down the hallway toward her room.

"Make it stop," Lindsey shrieked. "Mary Billingsworth, please make it stop! I wish for you to make this stop!"

Lindsey peered into the mirror, hoping to see her new wish come true.

It didn't happen.

What she saw instead was the granting of her original wish.

She watched in horrified silence as, one by one, the members of her family were sucked into Bloody Mary's mirror.

23

The house was silent.

The tornado was gone. And so was Lindsey's family.

There was nothing in the bathroom mirror now but Lindsey's own reflection.

But only for a second.

Lindsey stepped back in fear as a horrible face replaced her own.

Bloody Mary's piercing black eyes shot daggers through Lindsey, and her bloodred lips curled in a malicious sneer before they moved to form words.

Then Bloody Mary's voice came from the other

side of the mirror in a low hiss. "Now you are alone," she said as her image disappeared.

Suddenly, the door to the bathroom flew open.

Lindsey rushed from the room in a panic. As she stepped into the hallway, she cast a glance toward her bedroom. But she couldn't go in there—not alone. She was too afraid. She had to get help.

She raced down the stairs and out the door without looking back. Then she ran down the block toward Bree's house.

Lindsey was relieved to see that Tommy, Bree, and Ralphie were still outside, sitting on Bree's front lawn, talking.

"Something terrible has happened!" she screamed as she ran toward them.

The instant they saw her, they were all up on their feet, rushing to meet her.

"What's the matter?" Tommy asked as he reached her side.

Lindsey's mouth moved, but she couldn't make the words come out.

"Calm down," Bree soothed, putting a hand on Lindsey's arm.

"We have to do something!" Lindsey cried.

"First you have to tell us what happened," Tommy said.

"Bloody Mary," Lindsey answered him. "Bloody Mary took my family away."

Lindsey took a deep breath, trying to clear her head. She wanted to be able to explain as quickly as she could.

"I had a terrible fight with my parents over the mirror," she started, her voice quivering. "I ran upstairs and locked myself in the bathroom to get away from them." She paused to take a breath, ashamed to admit what she'd done next.

"Go on," Bree urged.

"They were yelling at me to come out. And I said, 'I wish you would all just leave me alone.'"

Her friends gasped.

"No!" Bree said.

Lindsey nodded.

"What happened then?" Tommy wanted to know.

"You're not going to believe this," Lindsey told them. She still didn't believe it herself. "A tornado came out of Mary Billingsworth's mirror and sucked them all in. Now they're stuck inside the mirror."

"We've got to get them out," Bree declared.

"What if we break the mirror?" Ralphie suggested.

"No," Lindsey said quickly. "If we break the mirror and they don't come out, what then?"

"Lindsey's right," Tommy agreed. "We can't break them out. We're going to have to wish them out."

Lindsey shook her head sadly. "It won't work," she explained. "I've already tried. The minute I realized what I'd said, I tried to undo the wish. It didn't work."

Tommy was undaunted. "Maybe Mary Billingsworth won't undo wishes," he reasoned. "But maybe she'll grant us a new one."

"Maybe," Lindsey said weakly.

The last thing in the world she wanted to do was call up Bloody Mary again. But she knew they had to do it. It was their only hope.

24

"No way I'm going back to Lindsey's," Ralphie informed them. "What if Bloody Mary sucks us into the mirror, too? Then what?"

"She's not going to suck us into the mirror," Tommy said. "Not unless we wish for it."

"How do you know?" Ralphie said. "Maybe Bloody Mary is just making up her own wishes now. After all, Lindsey didn't say 'I wish you'd suck my whole family into your mirror, Mary Billingsworth!' But she did it, didn't she?"

"Ralphie's got a point," Bree told them.

"Look!" Lindsey shouted. Time was ticking away,

and she wasn't about to waste any more of it. "If you guys don't want to come with me, I'll go back there myself. Tommy's right. The only chance I have of getting my family out of that mirror is to wish them out. And if you guys don't want to help me, I'll do it alone."

Lindsey was hoping that at least one of her friends would follow as she turned and headed down Bree's driveway. Luckily, one of them did.

"We're not letting you go back there alone," Tommy insisted, grabbing Lindsey's arm to stop her. "We're all coming with you. Aren't we, guys?"

Ralphie and Bree exchanged looks. But they didn't say a word. And they didn't make a move.

"Fine," Tommy snapped. "You don't have to come. You can just stand here like a couple of chickens. But after we get Lindsey's family out of that mirror, I'm sending Mary Billingsworth down here to get you!"

Ralphie gulped. "You wouldn't dare."

"Try me," Tommy said. Then he turned and stormed down the driveway, pulling Lindsey along with him.

"You're not really going to do that?" Lindsey whispered.

Tommy shook his head. "No," he muttered. "But Ralphie doesn't know that."

A moment later, Ralphie and Bree were so close behind them, they were stepping on Tommy's sneakers.

"Wait a minute, guys," Ralphie said. "I have a better idea."

"What?" Tommy said.

"Why can't we just wish them out of a different mirror?" Ralphie asked. "Like this one right here." He stopped by the side of Bree's father's car, and peered into the side-view mirror. "Hey, Bloody Mary," Ralphie called out nervously. "We wish Lindsey's family would come out of this mirror!"

Tommy and Lindsey stared at him in disbelief.

"Are you a total moron?" Tommy shouted. "Tom Thumb couldn't even fit through that mirror, much less two adults and a seven-year-old! Besides which, did Bloody Mary suck Lindsey's family into a car mirror? No! She sucked them into her mirror. So that's where we have to go to suck them back out again! Now are you coming or what?"

"Okay, okay," Ralphie grumbled. "I just thought it might work."

"Well, it didn't," Tommy said.

When they reached the sidewalk, Lindsey started to run. "Come on," she called over her shoulder. "We have to hurry!"

Tommy, Ralphie, and Bree took off behind her. But Ralphie and Bree stopped dead the moment they hit Lindsey's porch.

"Maybe we should get a couple of ropes to tie around our waists before we go in there," Ralphie suggested. "Just in case she starts sucking again."

"Yeah," Bree agreed. "We can tie them around the telephone pole down here so that she can't pull us into the mirror."

"I don't have ropes that long," Lindsey told them. "Besides, the wind in that house was worse than a tornado. If Bloody Mary wanted to suck us up, she could probably blow down the telephone pole, too."

That was hardly the news Ralphie and Bree wanted

to hear. As Lindsey opened the front door, the two of them almost got into a fistfight over who was going to walk through the door last.

Ralphie finally won, swearing to Bree that he would hold on to the back of her sweatshirt. That way, if anything started to suck, he could pull her away from it.

Lindsey couldn't believe Bree agreed. She was sure that if Ralphie felt even a breeze from the windows, the only thing he'd be trying to pull out of that house was his own butt.

"You want me to go in first?" Tommy asked Lindsey.

Lindsey shook her head. "No. But everybody keep quiet until we get upstairs, in case Bloody Mary is listening. There's a mirror right inside the foyer, and I don't want any more accidents."

The rest of them nodded their heads in agreement.

Lindsey held her breath as she stepped into the foyer with Tommy, Bree, and Ralphie in a single line behind her.

As the four of them climbed the stairs, the only sound to be heard was their rapid, strained breathing.

And as they headed for Lindsey's room, even that suddenly stopped.

From outside the door, Lindsey could see the mirror looming in the corner of her bedroom, waiting. "Listen," she said in a whisper. "The minute we see our reflections, I'm going to make the wish. Okay?"

"Why can't we just wait at the door?" Ralphie whispered back.

"You can if you want," Tommy told him. "But I wouldn't."

"Why not?" Bree asked.

"Because so far, standing in front of the mirror's been pretty safe," he told her. "It's only the people who *aren't* in front of the mirror who seem to get hurt."

That was all the convincing Ralphie and Bree needed.

"Ready?" Lindsey asked.

The other three nodded.

Please, please, please let this work, Lindsey begged as she slowly and cautiously headed for the mirror, with her friends right behind her.

She was almost afraid to look at the glass, afraid that she might see something even worse happening to her family inside the mirror than had happened to them outside. But as she finally took a step closer and caught sight of her face, she saw that the mirror was just as it had been before—vacant.

The moment Tommy, Ralphie, and Bree were reflected, Lindsey blurted her wish. "I wish my mom and my dad and Alyssa would come out of the mirror!"

Lindsey held her breath as she peered into the glass, waiting for a sign that her wish had been granted. But the faces staring back at her weren't the faces of her family. They were hers, Ralphie's, Tommy's, and Bree's.

"It didn't work," Lindsey cried, turning away from the mirror. "They're not coming out." She could feel the warm tears suddenly roll down her cheeks.

"We can't give up just like that," Tommy told her. "Maybe if we say the chant again, and *I* say the wish, it will work."

"Tommy's right," Bree said, trying to comfort Lindsey.

"We have to try again. And Tommy *should* make the wish. He's the only one who hasn't wished for anything yet."

"Could we get away from you-know-who while we're talking about this?" Ralphie asked, nodding his head toward the mirror and side-stepping his way toward the door.

The rest of them followed.

"Let's do this the right way," Bree insisted. "With the chant and the candle and everything. And I think we should probably call Bloody Mary by her real name— now that we know who she is."

"Oh, man," Ralphie moaned. "You've got to be kidding me."

"We have to, Ralphie," Bree told him. "It's the only thing left to try."

Lindsey knew that was true. And if it didn't work, she really *would* be left alone—forever.

"It's going to work," Tommy promised her as they finally positioned themselves back around the mirror.

"I hope so," Lindsey said, lighting the candle.

"Ready?" Bree asked.

Lindsey nodded. And as they started the chant, Lindsey was already wishing up a storm.

Mary Billingsworth is your name,
Please appear and play this game.
For the wish we ask of you,
You must make it now come true.
Once the wish has been revealed,
Can't turn back, its fate is sealed.
In return for what you give,
We will let your spirit live.

For Lindsey, the seconds that followed felt like an eternity. Then the glass started to haze and the hideous face of evil appeared.

Lindsey felt Ralphie and Bree nudge her in the side as if they needed to point out the horrifying image.

Tommy was just about to speak up when Lindsey blurted out the wish. "I wish that everyone would come out of the mirror!" she shouted. And as Lindsey stared into the haunted eyes of the spirit glaring back at her, Mary Billingsworth smiled maliciously.

Suddenly, the room turned cold. Lindsey felt as if she were standing outside in the dead of winter. She could even see her own breath drifting around her.

Before anyone could react, a blinding light shot out from the glass. Lindsey closed her eyes quickly. Her pupils felt as if they'd just been burned with a blowtorch. As she reached up to shield her eyes with her hands, a fierce, swirling force sent her flying across the room.

The only thing Lindsey could hear above the sound of her friends screaming was the sound of glass exploding around them.

25

W hat happened?" Tommy asked as he sat on the floor in a daze.

"I don't know," Lindsey mumbled, rubbing her eyes. She felt as though she'd been knocked out cold and was just now coming to.

"Look at the mirror!" Ralphie exclaimed.

Only the frame was intact. The glass had shattered into a million pieces that covered the floor of Lindsey's bedroom. The reflective surface was completely destroyed.

And Lindsey's parents and sister were nowhere to be seen.

"I should have let you make the wish," Lindsey told Tommy as she started to cry again. "Now what are we going to do?"

No one had an answer.

Lindsey's sobs echoed in the silence.

Then, suddenly, they heard something.

"Shhh," Bree said, moving to put a comforting arm around Lindsey. "Listen."

When Lindsey managed to quiet herself, she heard voices drifting up from downstairs.

Lindsey was up on her feet in an instant. She ran out into the hallway and toward the stairs. "Mom?" she screamed. "Is that you?"

"Lindsey?" her mother's voice came back at her.

"Are Dad and Alyssa down there with you?" Lindsey called hopefully.

"Of course they are," her mother said, sounding a little confused by the question. "What are you doing upstairs?" her mother asked. "I thought you went out for a walk with your friends."

"We did it!" Bree shrieked with glee. "They're out of the mirror!"

"Way to go!" Ralphie high-fived Tommy.

"It's like they don't remember a thing," Lindsey said happily.

Only Tommy looked worried. "How are you going to explain the broken mirror to your mom?" he asked Lindsey.

"Who cares?" she said. And she meant it. She'd make something up, say it was an accident. The worst that would happen was that she would get grounded for a while. It was a small price to pay to get Bloody Mary out of their lives.

The four friends headed down the stairs. Tommy took the lead, followed by Ralphie, then Bree. Lindsey glanced back at her bedroom and heaved a sigh of relief before following them.

At the bottom of the stairs, Tommy stopped abruptly.

"Oh, no," Ralphie gasped, coming to a halt behind Tommy.

Bree stopped too, letting out a muffled cry of dismay.

All three of them stood staring straight ahead into the mirror at the bottom of the stairs.

"What's wrong?" Lindsey asked as she pulled up short behind them.

They didn't have to reply. Lindsey saw it for herself. The answer was reflected in the mirror in front of them.

"Bloody Mary!" she gasped.

But this time, Mary Billingsworth wasn't looking at them from inside the mirror. She was standing behind them on the stairs.

Lindsey's blood ran cold as an icy hand gripped her shoulder.

"Your wish has come true," Mary Billingsworth whispered in her ear. "*Everyone* is out of the mirror now."

Lindsey started to scream, but terror choked the sound before it escaped her throat.

Tommy, Ralphie, and Bree stood paralyzed by the sight.

"Any *final* wishes?"

Lindsey felt Bloody Mary's breath swirling around her neck like a noose.

"The game is over," Mary Billingsworth continued. "Your time is up."

Lindsey was sure that was true—until she caught sight of Bloody Mary's reflection in the mirror. Suddenly, the face of evil was beginning to change.

Lindsey watched in amazement as Mary Billingsworth started to age.

Within seconds, the long dark hair that swirled around Bloody Mary's face and filled the mirror's frame was turning gray, while Bloody Mary's porcelain-white skin yellowed like bile and shriveled like a prune.

Tommy, Ralphie, and Bree gasped at the sight.

"I don't think she can survive outside of the mirror!" Tommy exclaimed.

Lindsey was hoping that was true as she pulled herself free from Bloody Mary's weakening grip. She spun around to address the evil face-to-face. "It looks like *your* time is up!" Lindsey told Bloody Mary as she pointed to the mirror.

Bloody Mary laughed—until she saw her reflection.

"*Noooooooo!*" Bloody Mary's cry was clear. But the words that followed were not.

Lindsey watched as Mary Billingsworth raised her

arms and commanded the mirror in a language that was unrecognizable.

Within seconds, Mary Billingsworth disappeared into thin air.

A moment later, the mirror cracked. Lindsey and her friends looked at one another and shivered.

The game was far from over.

Don't miss the next spine-tingling book
in the DEADTIME STORIES™ series

THE BEAST OF BASKERVILLE

Adam Riley started to sweat as he and his best friend, Eugene Nazzaro, slowly approached the long gravel drive that snaked its way up to the creepy old house on the hill. It was the Leeds house, where the Beast of Baskerville had been born, the house where the sniveling, snorting, subhuman creature lived now.

From the street, Adam could see all the warning signs telling him to turn tail and run. They were nailed to the rotted-out trees that lined the drive:

KEEP OUT! PRIVATE PROPERTY!

NO TRESPASSING ALLOWED!

ENTER AT YOUR OWN RISK!

BEWARE! THE BEAST OF BASKERVILLE IS WATCHING YOU!

Adam swallowed hard. The last thing in the world he wanted to do was climb Deadman's Hill.

But the creature was expecting him.

Here goes nothing, Adam thought, taking a deep breath to steady his nerves. He lifted his foot and crossed over the imaginary safety line between Ridge Road and the Leeds driveway.

Behind him, Eugene stopped dead in his tracks.

"This is not a good idea," Eugene told Adam for the twelve millionth time. "You're only asking for trouble."

"But if I don't deal with this now, I'm dead tonight!" Adam exclaimed.

"And what are you going to do when the little beast throws a big fat tizzy fit?" Eugene asked. "That's what will happen, you know—the minute you tell him you're not coming to his stupid birthday party tonight."

Adam knew Eugene was right.

J. J. Leeds, the thirteen-year-old, sniveling, snorting, subhuman creature that had moved into the Beast of Baskerville's old house, was definitely going to throw a major tizzy fit. Especially when he found out that *no one* in the neighborhood was planning to come to his party.

"You're not going to tell J.J. about anyone else, are you?" Eugene wanted to know.

"Are you nuts?" Adam shot back. "Then I'll really be dead. Because everyone in the neighborhood will kill me!"

Adam didn't even want to tell J.J. that he wasn't coming to the party, but thanks to his mom, he didn't have a choice.

Mrs. Riley felt sorry for J. J. Leeds. She insisted that the only reason all the neighborhood kids picked on him was because his last name was Leeds, just like the Beast's.

Adam had tried to explain to his mother that the

problem with J.J. wasn't his name at all. Lots of people in Baskerville were named Leeds, including Stacey Leeds, one of Adam's good friends. The Leeds family had founded the town of Baskerville more than two hundred years ago, and dozens of Leedses were still scattered about.

It wasn't even the fact that J.J. and his mom had moved into the creepiest house in town that made him a spitball target. If J.J. had been a normal kid, everyone in the neighborhood, except for Eugene, probably would have thought that was cool.

But J.J. wasn't a normal kid. He was a sniveling, snorting, loogie-spitting little beast. And everyone in the neighborhood knew it. Everyone but Mrs. Riley.

"I can't believe your mom is making you do this," Eugene said.

"Me neither," Adam groaned. "But if I don't tell J.J. face-to-face that I'm not coming to his party later, my mom won't let me sleep out tonight. And if I don't give him this stupid present, she'll make me go to his party."

"So why don't you just leave the present in the mailbox and tell your mom he wasn't home?" Eugene suggested.

Adam considered that idea for a second. But he knew it wouldn't work. "I can't," he told Eugene. "My mom might call Mrs. Leeds. Then I'll really be in trouble."

J.J.'s mom was always at home. She didn't own a car, and she rarely went out.

J.J. claimed that Mrs. Leeds had to stay inside because she was allergic to the air on the outside.

No one believed it. Mrs. Leeds was just creepy, and another reason no one wanted to go to J.J.'s party.

"So what do you want to do?" Eugene asked, cringing. "Talk to Mrs. Leeds?"

Adam shot him a look. "No, I don't want to talk to Mrs. Leeds! But if my mom does, she'll know I didn't even ring the doorbell."

None of the kids in the neighborhood had ever even seen Mrs. Leeds since she and J.J. moved in, except through the windows of her house. She was usually up in the "Beast Tower," sitting in front of the stained-glass window, rocking back and forth in her chair, watching to make sure no one stepped foot on her property.

It was Mrs. Leeds who'd put up all the warning signs to keep the neighborhood kids out.

"Oh, man." Eugene sighed. "This is a nightmare."

"Tell me about it," Adam agreed.

"Why's your mother being such a bed bug about this anyway?" Eugene wondered.

"Because she feels bad that J.J. doesn't have any friends in the neighborhood," Adam explained. "And she doesn't want me to be mean."

"Yeah, well, J.J. doesn't have any friends *outside* the neighborhood, either," Eugene pointed out.

"I know," Adam said. "But my mom thinks that's because Mrs. Leeds didn't send him to school, not because he's a booger ball."

"Mrs. Leeds didn't *have* to send him to school, remember?" Eugene mocked. "J.J.'s a genius."

"Yeah, right." Adam smirked. "J.J.'s a real genius. He doesn't even know his first name."

He didn't, either. J.J. insisted that the J's were his name, not just initials.

"No way that kid has a three thousand I.Q.," Eugene said, shaking his head.

"No kidding," Adam said. "I.Q.'s don't even go up that high, you moron. He made that up."

But J.J. had sworn it was true. He claimed he was so smart, he didn't have to go to school.

"Let's just get this over with," Adam said impatiently, taking a step up the drive.

"Sorry, pal." Eugene's feet were still planted on the safe side of the imaginary line. "From here on in, you're on your own. No way I'm climbing Deadman's Hill."

"It's just a driveway," Adam huffed.

"Oh, yeah?" Eugene shot back. "Tell that to the Beast of Baskerville's victims."

"That's just a stupid legend," Adam told him.

"Then how come everyone knows this is the Beast's house?" Eugene demanded.

"*Was* his house," Adam corrected, "more than two hundred years ago. And no one knows that for sure."

"*Everyone* knows that for sure," Eugene protested. "And everyone knows this is the hill he dragged all his victims up—right before he tore them to shreds and buried them in his well."

"What well?" Adam asked. "Do you see a well on this property?"

"Nooooo," Eugene replied. "But that doesn't mean it's not here."

Adam stared at Eugene. Apparently, J.J. wasn't the only genius in the neighborhood. "If you can't *see* the well, then how can it be here?"

"Maybe it's hidden," Eugene suggested.

Adam rolled his eyes. "How the heck do you hide a three-thousand-pound tunnel made out of stone?"

"Who knows," Eugene answered. "When witches are involved, anything is possible."

"What witches?" Adam asked, exasperated.

"The witches that cursed Elvira," Eugene told him. "The ones that turned Jimmy Leeds into the Beast before he was born."

Elvira Leeds was supposedly the Beast of Baskerville's mother. She was also a witch. According to legend, Elvira Leeds married a mortal back in the 1700s when the town of Baskerville was first founded. And because she broke the rules of her coven, which stated that witches could marry only warlocks, the other witches cursed her. They turned her husband into a three-headed newt with one eye. Then they put a spell on her unborn child.

When Elvira Leeds finally gave birth to her son, Jimmy, he was only half human. His arms and legs were normal, but the rest of him was beastly.

Two twisted horns shot out of his skull, while two goatlike hooves grew in place of ten human toes. His eyes burned red like flames. And every inch of his body was covered with matted black hair.

Jimmy Leeds was supposedly so hideous that his witchy mother tossed him down the well on her property, hoping to be rid of him.

But Jimmy Leeds didn't die. Instead, he grew into the Beast. Rumor had it that every so often, Jimmy Leeds had climbed out of the well to feed on innocent children.

Some people, like Eugene, believed he still did.

"You know what?" Adam sighed in frustration. "You're a yo-yo. There is no well. And there's no Beast of Baskerville, either. Now are you coming with me or what? Because if you don't come with me, I'll tell J.J. about tent night tonight," he threatened.

"You wouldn't dare!" Eugene turned pale.

"Would, too," Adam lied. "And I'll tell everyone that *you're* the one who told him."

"Tent night" was another reason no one wanted to go to J.J.'s party. All the kids in the neighborhood had been planning to sleep out for weeks. They were all setting up tents in their backyards. Then, when the parents were in bed for the night, the kids were going to sneak out of their yards to play kick-the-can and hang out.

Needless to say, J.J. wasn't invited.

"I mean it," Adam bluffed. "And I'll tell J.J. you want him to sleep in our tent."

Eugene gave in. "I'll go with you, okay?" he agreed in a panic. "But if something bad happens to us on this hill, I'm blaming you."

"Nothing bad is going to happen to us," Adam assured him.

But Adam was wrong.

Something bad *was* going to happen to them—but not on the hill.

189

About the Authors

As sisters, Annette and Gina Cascone share the same last name. As writers, they sometimes share the same brain. As children, they found it difficult to share anything at all.

The Cascone sisters grew up in Lawrenceville, New Jersey. It was there that Annette and Gina began making up stories. Since their father was a criminal attorney, and their mother claimed to have ESP, the Cascone sisters honed their storytelling skills early on in life—mainly to stay out of trouble. These days, they're telling their crazy stories to anyone who will listen.

Here are the stats: Gina is older; Annette is not. Gina is married; Annette should be. Gina has two children; Annette borrowed one. Gina has a granddaughter; Annette has a grandniece. Gina has cats; Annette has dogs. They both have a sister named Elise.

Visit Annette and Gina at www.agcascone.com.

DEADTIME STORIES

Starring Disney's *Wizards of Waverly Place* JENNIFER STONE *as the* Babysitter